AUSTIN BROWER

The Vale Machine

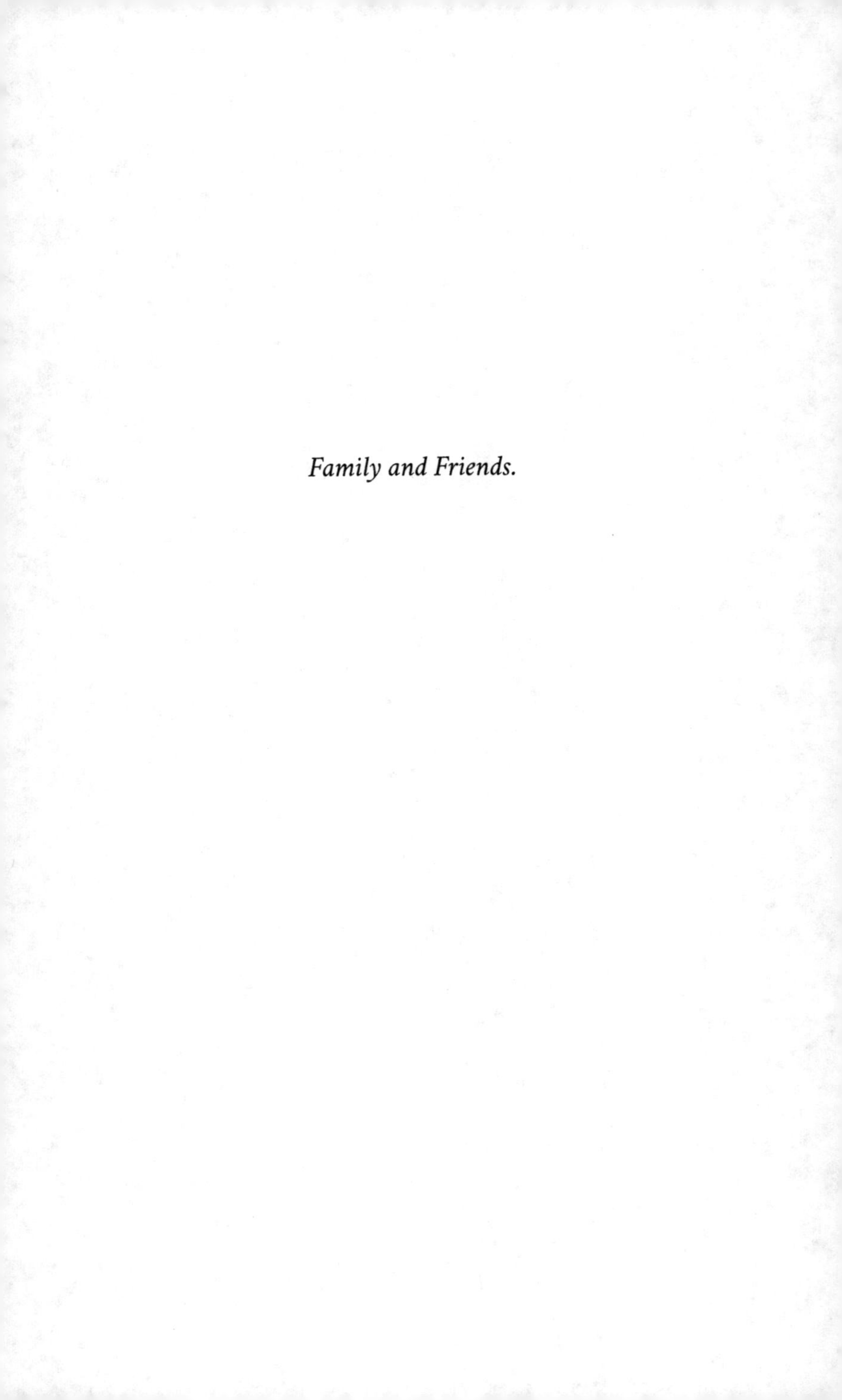

Family and Friends.

Contents

Foreword

"In "The Vale Machine," author Austin Brower takes us on a riveting journey as he explores the implications of creating a way to time travel. The story follows three young scientists who are striving to help cure diseases and sicknesses through the use of a device they have built, only to be undermined by a formidable and unlikely foe. This fast-paced adventure introduces elements of action, comedy, and intimacy, with unexpected surprises from beginning to end. You will find yourself emotionally enthralled by the plight of Silas and his friends as they work against time and powerful enemies to safeguard their creation." -Charlie Amicangelo

Preface

Writing this book has been a roller coaster of emotions—from moments of frustration and doubt to bursts of exhilaration and joy. There were times when I questioned every word, every plot twist, and every character choice. Yet, amidst the uncertainty, one thing remained constant: my unwavering passion for storytelling.

I wouldn't trade this journey for anything else. It has been a testament to perseverance, creativity, and the thrill of bringing worlds to life through words. This book, along with others I am currently crafting, has become a new and permanent passion that I am incredibly excited to share with you, dear reader.

Within these pages, you'll embark on a journey that explores the timeless battle between good and evil. You'll witness the depths to which people will sink in their hunger for power and control. But more than that, you'll discover the enduring strength of friendship—a force that transcends the pages of a story and echoes in the tapestry of our lives.

In a world where uncertainty looms large and challenges abound, believing in oneself becomes a beacon of hope. Through the characters and their trials, I hope to inspire you to embrace your own journey, trust in your abilities, and never underestimate the power of resilience.

As you turn the pages and immerse yourself in the world

I've created, I invite you to reflect on your own experiences, ponder the complexities of human nature, and find solace in the enduring truths that bind us all together.

Thank you for joining me on this adventure. Your presence, dear reader, gives meaning to these words and breathes life into these stories.

With gratitude,

Austin Brower

Acknowledgement

I would like to extend my deepest gratitude to my editor, Robin LeeAnn, for her tireless dedication and expertise in helping me shape this book. Her hard work and insightful feedback have been instrumental in bringing out the best in my writing.

I am also immensely grateful to both old and new friends who have stood by my side throughout this journey. Your unwavering support, encouragement, and friendship have meant the world to me. Thank you for believing in me and sharing in the excitement while I start this new journey.

The Prologue

2046

Nestled deep within the sprawling suburbs of Dallas, Texas, an inconspicuous facility held the world's most profound secret— a secret with the potential to mend the past and shape the future. It was here that Silas, Amelia, and Jesse toiled tirelessly, their hearts and minds devoted to a contraption known as The Machine.

Amid rows of sterile lab rooms and bustling corridors, the trio honed their creation, a time travel device conceived to transcend boundaries. The world had known revolutions in science and technology, but nothing as audacious as this. The Machine was a marvel—a conduit through which they could peer into time, a tool for healing and understanding.

For years, they had labored, guided by noble intentions. They sought to alleviate human suffering by seeing how medicines would affect people three decades hence and ensuring safer, more effective treatments. Whenever a new pharmaceutical breakthrough emerged, The Machine would unravel its mysteries.

But as whispers of their work spread, so did the shadows of two formidable adversaries.

One was the president—an enigmatic figure who wields power as vast as the oceans and ambitions as boundless as the cosmos. He saw The Machine not as a tool of healing but as a lever to mold history, an instrument to reshape destinies.

The other adversary was the Cult of the Sacred Bodies, a mysterious sect. They feared the tampering of time, viewing The Machine as an affront to the natural order. For them, it was a blasphemous act, a wicked foray into domains that mere mortals should never tread.

Silas, Amelia, and Jesse knew not the extent of these adversaries' influence nor the depths of their commitment. They only understood that their creation held the power to either change the world or plunge it into chaos. But the whispers of time beckoned them, a siren's call filled with hope and trepidation.

In the heart of Texas, where history intertwined with the future, The Machine softly hummed. Its ethereal glow illuminated the dimly lit facility—a symbol of hope and peril, of healing and destruction

The First Chapter: The Age of the Cornucopia

1625

In the heart of the dense forest, beneath the towering canopies, the poultry gathered in secret. Among them, Turk stood tall, a broad chested turkey, his long sturdy espresso brown feathers rustling in the wind as he addressed the assembly.

"Fellow poultry," he began, his voice unwavering. "For far too long, we have suffered under the tyranny of these giants. Our peaceful kingdom has turned into a realm of fear and suffering. But today, we stand united, ready to take back what is rightfully ours."

Heads nodded as the assembly softly clucked in unity.

"We might be considered simple creatures by their standards, but we possess a strength that comes from unity—from our bonds with one another and from the very land we inhabit. Our determination and cunningness will be our greatest weapons. We have learned their ways and studied their tactics, and now it is time to turn the tables."

Turk's eyes gleamed as he continued. "We will show them that we are not to be underestimated. Our ambush will strike like lightning, catching them off guard and tearing through their ranks. We have the element of surprise, and the eagles will be our silent, lethal companions, swooping down from above and striking terror into their hearts."

The assembly burst into excited clucks and flapping of wings. The majestic eagles, who were perched nearby, had their sharp eyes fixed on Turk as if they understood every word he spoke.

Turk's beak curled into a determined smile. "Our armory, crafted from our very surroundings, may be rudimentary, but it carries the weight of our resilience and determination. Stones that have borne witness to our suffering will now serve as projectiles against our oppressors. The wood that once sheltered us will now strike them down."

Amid the crowd, a wise old owl hooted in approval, its eyes glowing.

"We march toward victory, my comrades. For this is not just a battle of flesh and feathers, but a battle of spirit and freedom. As we gather our forces and prepare for the coming storm, remember this: our courage is mightier than any weapon, and our unity shall be our strength."

With that, the assembly erupted into a chorus of clucks and flaps. The sound resonated through the forest, a testament to their unwavering resolve.

Turk led his comrades toward the battle against the giants with an unshakable determination. The fight for freedom was on the horizon.

On a hillside, Turk sat, overlooking the future battle. The weight of the battle, before it even started, weighed on him. He thought back to the blood that had been shed the previous years, when the giants had raided their homes and murdered their loved ones.

Aerowyn Swiftshadow, a wise old great horned owl, who

was brown and white chested, big yellow eyes, and Turk's best friend, fluttered and landed next to Turk. Despite being much older than the other fowl, his vision remained sharper than his companions. He rotated his head toward Turk. "Do you believe this year will be the year we reclaim what was ravaged by those monsters?"

Turk gazed into the distance, his mind still wandering to the past. He was young then but old enough to comprehend the unfolding tragedy, to feel the anguish, and to yearn for retribution. "Yes," he replied, his voice laced with determination. "This will be the year. Yet we must acknowledge that we can never fully restore what has been stolen. We may never reunite with our beloved ones, but we can grant them the vengeance they deserve—a swift and merciless reckoning."

Turk looked over the cliff's edge, waiting. The giants' distraction had been set the night before. He had led the rabbits into the giants' fields to destroy as many crops as possible. That should let the rest of the poultry group move in from the south undetected.

Turk gave a gobble which is the signal to Aerowyn, who conveyed it to the fowl ranks. Group by group, they descended the hill to take up their attack positions. Within forty-five minutes, every bird was in place in the sky and behind the tree line, and the assault began.

They went from house to house, attacking as many giants as possible. Yet these bewildered giants were much stronger than Turk had anticipated. They swiftly reached for their weapons of destruction, aimed, and picked off the birds one by one.

At the front line of the attack, Turk faced the armed giants with his claws out and chest puffed. The giants' weapons cracked like lightning, causing his ears to feel like they were exploding.

Time seemed to slow as he witnessed the slaughter of his allies. However, this didn't deter Turk. He aimed for the giants' legs, trying to take them down. He swooped down to attack one giant's knee, but the giant swung his leg back, and he missed. The leg came back around and kicked his ribs, cracking several. He slammed against a wall of a barn, and the world went black.

Voices Turk had never heard before spoke, but he didn't understand what they were saying. A ringing soon drowned the voices out, and the ground shook.

Slowly, he opened his eyes. A bright light overwhelmed him, but eventually, his vision came into focus. What were once black blurs were his people still fighting these giants.

A continuous screech so foul echoed above, and Turk looked up. The wise old owl fell from the sky, bleeding from his right wing. He fell so fast that there was no way to slow him down. With a crash, he landed on a pile of branches which splintered under him.

The screeching stopped.

As challenging as it already was to breathe, the pain of seeing his best friend immobile, blood spilling onto a pile of branches, took Turk's breath away. Pain tore right through him.

He knew this had to stop now.

Slowly, Turk got to his feet and charged toward the nearest giant. He aimed his beak for the back of the giant's leg, grabbed onto the back of the giant's knee, and used his feet to shred whatever he could. The giant fell, screaming, which either made Turk laugh from the joy of revenge or from his overwhelming pain.

He loosened his grip and moved on to the next giant. One

after another, he managed to take down four giants. Blood and tendons now covered him. Catching his breath, he looked around and saw that the eagles had joined in from above, attacking not only the new giants who looked different and unfamiliar, but also those who were present before. The eagles went for the giants' heads, attempting to reach their eyes and whatever else their talons could grasp.

As Turk turned around the corner, a warmth spread in his chest. He brushed it aside, attributing it to the exertion of running and fighting. Spotting his next target, he sprinted after the giant. However, his vision darkened, and it felt as if he was darting through a tunnel. His breathing grew heavier, and he slowed to a near trot.

Voices spoke again. Clearer this time. Familiar. He finally could comprehend what they were saying.

"Come back to us before it's too late!" one said.

Turk believed they must be either in his head or perhaps the voices of the fallen poultry from years ago.

He fell, his head striking the dirt. He tried to take in a deep breath but could barely manage to fill his lungs with air. It seemed like liquid flowed where air should be. He attempted to rise, but his strength gave way, and he lay there with his head turned to the side.

"Not yet! He's not ready to come to us yet. He's so close."

Turk tried to disregard the voices, though they sounded so incredibly familiar.

Looking around once more, he barely lifted his head. Bodies were scattered everywhere—his family, his friends, and everyone who had placed their trust in him. All gone.

Lying there, he breathed in whatever air he could, but only dust from the ground filled his lungs. His vision grew even darker, and he tried to recollect every significant event in his life. However, only images of his family and the massacre came to mind. Over and over. He thought about his best friend, attempting to summon memories of the good times, but all he could visualize was his friend's fall.

His vision went black. Nothing.

Then silence.

"Silas, wake up."

The Second Chapter: Awake

"Silas, wake up," a voice—faint yet stern—whispered again.

Silas's head pounded as he attempted to open his eyes, but due to the consuming migraine, he couldn't. He ended up passing out again due to the pain.

"We shouldn't have let him stay there for so long," a woman in her midthirties said in a gentle voice. She was rather tall compared to other women she knew, although not towering. Her dark brown hair had blonde streaks, and numerous freckles accompanied her light tan. "There could be serious complications. He might not even remember who he is!"

"We shouldn't have allowed him to undertake this endeavor from the beginning, Amelia, especially when he knew the potential consequences of staying in for too long," a man in his late forties said, standing across from her. Though he didn't appear his age, looking much younger. His sandy brown hair and ungroomed beard gave him a rugged appearance. While lacking a six-pack, he remained quite fit.

"I know. I know…" Her expression remained resolute. She had known the risks involved, but the potential gains had outweighed them. Despite the circumstances, her determination to uncover the truth had driven her to take calculated risks.

Amelia checked the equipment one last time to make sure

Silas was in good condition. She then sat in the chair across from the bed where he was hooked up to the machine bed.

The bed's structure was a harmonious blend of futuristic elegance and functional precision. The metallic ring that encircled Silas's head radiated a soft, pulsating glow, casting an otherworldly light upon him. Its cables branched out like a mind's neural pathways, converging in a symphony of connections with colossal computers and intricate machinery that adorned the walls. A network of fine wires also extended from his body to the machinery. These machines hummed together with purpose, orchestrating a symphony of data and electrical impulses.

Jesse, her coworker, got up from the chair next to her. It was getting late into the afternoon, and he decided to go pick up food for them.

After he left, only the constant hum of machinery and the scent of sterile equipment filled the dimly lit room. The research facility was a world of its own, where time often blurred.

Amelia looked at Silas once more, her eyes filled with a mixture of concern and affection. He was the same age as her, and they had known each other since they were twenty-five. He had dirty blond hair and a beard that added a hint of sophistication to his appearance. Physically, he wasn't the biggest or strongest guy around, but he exuded an air of quiet confidence that drew people toward him.

She returned her attention to her laptop, and the screen's headlines reminded her of the broader world outside the research facility. The news stories painted a vivid picture of humanities' complexities and uncertainties. Yet, in that moment, her thoughts were divided between the global issues on her screen and the concern she had for Silas.

Amelia looked up from her computer and gazed at him again. She recalled the long eight-year journey they had undertaken. Of sleepless nights. Of heated debates over algorithms and protocols. Of the countless revisions. It had all led them to this moment—a convergence of their passion and ingenuity.

Pride and excitement swelled her. This machine was more than a culmination of technology; it was the embodiment of their shared aspirations, the legacy they were carving.

This machine's primary purpose was to expedite humanity's understanding of medicine, condensing years of testing and experimentation into just a matter of hours. With its capabilities, it had the potential to revolutionize the progression of medicine—saving time, resources, and lives.

But it also carried the weight of ethical considerations and consequences of tampering with the natural progression of medical knowledge.

Footsteps sounded, and she looked toward the door. Jesse was back with brown bags and drinks.

"Anything happen yet?" he asked.

She shook her head.

He handed her a brown bag and sat in the chair next to her. She opened the bag and pulled out a wrapped, greasy cheeseburger and fries. He handed her her drink, which was an orange soda—her favorite.

"Things are getting wild out there, Amelia," he said between bites. "You would think their voices would have gone hoarse from yelling all day. I understand their point of view, but what we are doing could save millions of lives."

Amelia took a sip of her orange soda and looked out the one way glass window, where the fervent protesters continued to make their presence felt. Their signs were visible even from the room's confines. Though The Machine's humming drowned out their shouts.

The peaceful protests outside their facility had morphed into much more fervent chants that only grew stronger. All from the Cult of the Sacred Bodies. They saw themselves as guardians of a fundamental cosmic balance and believed what the trio was doing was a violation of the natural order—a defiance of the very laws governing life and death.

"It's a difficult line to walk," she replied, her voice tinged with a mix of frustration and understanding. "But they're missing the bigger picture."

Jesse nodded. "Absolutely."

Amelia glanced at Silas and then looked at Jesse. "Pioneers have always faced resistance. But we have science, reason, and a genuine desire to help humanity on our side. That has to count for something."

As they finished their meal, a renewed determination filled the room.

"What happened?" a hoarse voice came from the bed.

"He's awake," Amelia said as both her and Jesse rushed to the bed from the chairs across the room next to the window.

Light stinged Silas's eyes. As his vision refocused, he looked around. His memory was a bit hazy. "Where am I?"

"Silas, do you remember who you are? Or us?" Jesse asked.

He shook his head. "I feel like I know you both, but I can't put a name to your faces."

Amelia exchanged a concerned glance with Jesse. "It's all right, Silas," she said gently, her voice a mixture of reassurance and patience. "You've been through quite an experience. Your memory might take some time to fully come back."

Jesse nodded. "You've been connected to a machine. We've been working on a project together, a groundbreaking one."

Silas's brow furrowed as he tried to make sense of the information. A mixture of curiosity and confusion shifted inside him as if his mind was sifting through fragments of a dream he couldn't quite grasp.

As they spoke of this project and making alterations to it, Silas's gaze shifted from Jesse to Amelia. He took in their earnest expressions, their genuine concern in their eyes. A flicker of recognition stirred within him. Though the specifics still eluded him.

"Give it some time, Silas," Amelia continued. "Your memory will likely come back in pieces. We're here to help you through this process."

Silas offered her a tentative smile. "I appreciate that," he said softly. "I'm just…I'm just trying to piece everything together."

Jesse looked down at Silas seeing the concern on his face, placed a reassuring hand on his shoulder. "We're here for you every step of the way, my friend. We've got your back."

As Silas grappled with the fragments of his memory, a sense of growing trust in the people who stood by his side bloomed. They might not have all the answers just yet, but these two were a beacon of assurance amid the uncertainty.

The Third Chapter: Recollect

After a few moments of silence, Jesse bid his farewell for the night, preparing to spend some time with his wife and daughter before returning in the morning. They exchanged warm goodnight wishes, and the room settled into a calm stillness.

Amelia turned her attention to Silas, tending to his well-being with a quick check of his vitals and a thoughtful glass of water. His consumption of the water seemed almost desperate, as though he had been deprived for weeks and not hours.

Her concern was evident in her gaze. "You really don't remember much, do you?"

He subtly shook his head. "It feels a bit foggy, and I've got a migraine."

Her brow furrowed. "Well, we were worried that this might happen. Traveling through time puts a significant strain on your mind and subconscious. Fortunately, it didn't escalate any further."

Silas's eyes widened as the magnitude of his experience finally hit him like a wave. "I traveled through time?!"

His heart rate monitor accelerated, and he found himself breathing faster and more heavily.

"Silas, I need you to breathe," she said. "You've gone through something quite traumatic, and it's important to regulate your breathing."

His mind raced as he struggled to process the situation. Could it be real? Had he not witnessed the loss of his loved ones and rallied an army only to face failure—as a bird? What implications did that hold? Questions tumbled through his mind in a whirlwind of confusion.

Amelia's reassuring presence was a lifeline amid his tumultuous thoughts. Her calmness gave him something to hold onto as he attempted to navigate his storm of emotions. He closed his eyes and concentrated on his breathing, on each inhale and exhale. Gradually, his heart rate slowed, and the dizziness subsided.

But her words still echoed in his mind. The journey he had undergone *transcended* time. The gravity of the situation settled in, stirring a mix of awe, confusion, and hope.

As his breathing steadied, he reopened his eyes, meeting her gaze. "How is that possible? How could I have traveled through time?"

The room remained quiet, the humming machinery serving as the only audible backdrop. Amelia's and Silas's gazes locked in a shared moment of uncertainty and anticipation.

Drawing in a deep breath, Amelia's voice broke the stillness. "We figured it out, Silas. You, Jesse, and I cracked the code for time travel." Her words carried an undercurrent of awe and disbelief, as if even *she* couldn't fully fathom their achievement. "We conducted preliminary experiments using rats, although the results lacked precision. Thus, the decision was made for a human subject. We sent you back in time as a trial—both to assess the viability of human time travel and to glean invaluable insights. And now you, Silas, hold the distinction of being the inaugural time traveler."

As her revelation settled, the extraordinary moment suspended in time, offering a glimpse into a realm of possibilities that had solely existed in the realms of fiction and speculation until now.

Silas sat there after being unhooked from the machine, his thoughts still a whirlwind. His mental steps retraced the mysterious journey he had just undertaken. His mind struggled to grasp the authenticity of his experiences, questioning whether they were genuine or mere fragments of an elaborate dream. With every passing second, the line between reality and illusion blurred, leaving him in a state of bewilderment.

Amelia's attentive gaze remained fixed on him, her perceptive nature attuned to his internal struggle. His emotions were an open book to her, conveyed through the subtle play of his expressions.

"Silas, what's troubling you?" Worry filled her soft voice. "What happened during your time travel?"

He met her gaze, drawing in a deep breath. His words then wove a vivid tapestry of his experiences—scenes that had etched themselves onto his mind, emotions that had left their mark.

"It appears a mix-up occurred. Your intended destination was a man named"—she glanced at the clipboard for reference—"Thomas Folsom. Yet, somehow, you found yourself occupying the body of a turkey. An unexpected and quite intriguing turn of events." The edges of her lips curled into a suppressed smile.

Silas looked up, and a faint hue of embarrassment tinged her cheeks as she realized her response might have come across as lighthearted. They shared a laugh, a temporary respite from the complexities of their endeavor.

A moment of silence hung in the air before she pulled her chair closer to the side of his bed. She engaged in conversation, discussing the project and endeavoring to catch him up in the hopes that it might trigger his memory.

Yet one question remained for Silas. His gaze held a mixture of anticipation and uncertainty. "How long was I gone?"

"You were under for fourteen hours and twenty-three minutes before you returned and passed out."

He processed this information, the reality settling in. He sat there, grappling with the realization that although it felt like a lifetime for him, he had only been absent for slightly over half a day.

With a nod, they continued their conversation, delving deeper into the intricacies of his journey. A few hours slipped by unnoticed, and Amelia eventually succumbed to sleep. His gaze wandered over to her arm, noting the time on her watch—4:32 a.m. He deduced that Jesse would likely return in a few hours, prompting him to consider getting some rest as well.

After drifting into slumber, Silas's dreams took on a disjointed quality. Fragments of his time travel experiences intermingled with memories from his college years and the recent past. They shifted unpredictably—from being a turkey hunting for food to sitting at a desk alongside Amelia, engrossed in a research assignment. The boundaries between his various life phases blurred.

The vivid, heartbreaking moment when he had witnessed his best friend being shot down in the sky jolted him awake, his heart racing. The abrupt awakening was triggered by Jesse's entrance. Jesse paused where he stood, coffee and breakfast in his hands. Silas's phone dropped and clattered to the floor, a clang echoing in the room. Amelia stirred awake, stretching and wiping a small trace of dried drool from the side of her mouth. Silas and Jesse shared a chuckle at her expense while Jesse picked up the phone.

Jesse's arrival brought a renewed sense of comfort. Silas reveled in the warmth of his coffee, its rich aroma mingling with the flavors of his breakfast. What a stark contrast between this meal and the sustenance he had ingested as a turkey.

While he was engaged in his breakfast, Amelia seized the opportunity to provide Jesse with a comprehensive update—his life as a bird and his participation in a monumental war. Jesse sat back, captivated by the unfolding narrative. With each new revelation, he leaned in a bit more. Occasionally, Silas injected nuances and clarifications, adding layers to its complexity.

Driven by a mixture of intrigue and skepticism, Jesse reached for his phone, embarking on an internet search to uncover any historical references that might align with Silas's astonishing account. His search yielded a short story from 1625, recounting a peculiar incident where pilgrims and Native Americans had allegedly been besieged by a swarm of birds and small creatures during Thanksgiving. He looked up from his phone, and shared laughter filled the room. The notion that Silas's experiences might hold a historical parallel was both amusing and thought-provoking.

As their laughter subsided, a sense of camaraderie and accomplishment settled over them. The knowledge that their names were poised to be etched into history's pages resonated.

After a brief pause punctuated by the sounds of chewing, Jesse pivoted the conversation toward his daughter and wife. He retrieved a cherished photo of them and shared it with

Silas in a bid to spark his memory. Silas's gaze lingered on the image, a gentle smile playing at the corners of his lips.

The camaraderie they shared, the stories exchanged, and the rekindled bonds acted as catalysts, invoking memories from the depths of his consciousness. As he looked back at the photo in Jesse's hand, he realized that the journey he had undertaken had not only granted him insight into an avian alter ego but also provided him with a renewed appreciation for his own human experiences.

Amelia swiftly collected his discarded trash and disposed of it in the bin outside the room. With practiced efficiency, she and Jesse shifted their focus to the tangle of cables and the IV drip, methodically disconnecting them. With his gradual return to equilibrium, they freed him from the confines of the medical bed. She glanced at the clock, documenting the passage of time since Silas's awakening.

They then thoughtfully provided Silas with fresh clothing and aided him as he eased himself out of bed. He stood and moved without any discomfort. Respecting his privacy, they allowed him the space to change and prepare for the next phase.

Emerging from the privacy, he found Amelia and Jesse prepared for the next course of action: a series of mental tests. All to ensure his mental faculties were still intact.

Silas diligently tackled the battery of mental tests over the next few hours, to which Silas passed all of the tests. For lunch, Jesse and Amelia chose to treat him to his preferred Asian restaurant. After they gathered their belongings, they made their way toward the building's exit. However, as they drew near, the protesters' voices grew more pronounced.

Aware of the potential disturbance, Jesse turned to Silas. "Keep your focus ahead and follow me. We're heading directly to the parking garage."

Silas nodded, his heart rate slightly elevated from the unexpected tension. Stepping out, he maintained his gaze straight ahead, his steps guided by Jesse's lead. The protesters' chanting and clamor reverberated around them. The path to the parking garage seemed to stretch on longer than usual.

Upon reaching the parking garage, a collective breath of relief filled the air. The familiar hum of engines and the cool shade provided a contrast to the fervor outside.

As they made their way to Jesse's car, Silas couldn't help but reflect on the dissonance between the tranquility of their lunch plans and the tumultuous scene they had just navigated. The world around him remained as complex and unpredictable as ever.

Jesse started the car. At the garage exit, he scanned his badge and gained access to leave. As they merged onto the street, they found themselves amid a sea of protesters crowding the sidewalks. People shouted at the passing vehicles. Some even spat on the window next to Silas, who annoyed glanced at Jesse. The whole car shuttered as part of a brick struck the windshield.

"Shit!" Jesse yelled. "What the hell?!" He accelerated and maneuvered onto another street, leaving the chaotic scene behind.

For a while, silence enveloped the car, punctuated only by the faint hum of the engine and the occasional rustle of leaves brushing against the windows.

"Damn, man," Jesse remarked, breaking the quiet. "I just had that windshield fixed after last month's hailstorm."

The tension diffused with shared laughter of the absurdity of the situation.

The Thai restaurant had an unusual emptiness, considering it was the typical lunch rush hour. Yet they were one of only three cars in the parking lot. They exited the car and proceeded to the entrance. Curiously, no one stood at the podium to seat them. After a brief wait, a short, older woman rushed out, with menus in hand, and swiftly led them to their seats. She took their orders and headed back to the kitchen.

As they settled into their seats, their attention was drawn to a television in the corner of the room. The news was on.

"The Cult of the Sacred Bodies will be apprehended for their involvement in destroying research facilities across neighboring states," the news anchor reported. "Their actions were aimed at sabotaging the development of a time travel machine intended for medical research. President Jason King has declared the cult's escalating attacks a growing threat and has announced the deployment of his newly established in-country security unit, Control. He also designated the cult members as terrorists."

The weight of the news story hung in the air, casting a shadow over the already eventful day. They exchanged shocked and concerned looks.

"What if they come for us next?" Silas asked. "How do we protect ourselves?"

Before anyone could respond, footsteps grew nearer. Expecting the waitress, Silas turned around, only to find five imposing figures coming into view. These tall, muscular men were clad in what looked like red and black riot armor. He looked back at Jesse and Amelia. Fear was etched in her eyes, while Jesse's expression bore a mix of irritation and readiness.

The space between them widened as a man who easily stood over six feet tall emerged from behind the guards. He possessed a slender build. His thick hair was swept back and had a distinct gray streak running through it. His blue eyes gleamed with a cunning intensity, set against a powerful jawline.

He promptly seized the nearest chair, dragged it to their table, and seated himself. His gaze swept across the trio, and the intensity in his eyes made it feel as though he could peer into their very souls.

"Lady and gentlemen, I'm sure my identity isn't a mystery to you, so let's keep things informal," he began. "You can call me Jason. First and foremost, I'd like to extend my congratulations for your successful time travel endeavors. I've heard there were minor hitches, but those can surely be sorted out. Mr. Silas Vale, your courage doesn't go unnoticed. You're now the Armstrong of time—a true pioneer."

Heavy silence enveloped them as he held Silas's gaze. Eventually, his hand extended for a handshake, and Silas gradually reciprocated the gesture.

"Now, for an achievement like this, the three of you should celebrate, albeit somewhere more suitable than this place." His gaze swept around the room with a slightly disgusted expression. "I also want to assure you that I'll be stationing around your research facility to safeguard you from those individuals in the streets. What a waste of space."

His tone shifted to a more serious note. "I'm also curious about the broader potential of the machine beyond medicine. Some colleagues of mine share that curiosity. Perhaps we can arrange a visit to explore its other applications."

Rising from his seat, he picked up Silas's glass, took a sip, and set it down. "Well, I'll be in touch. Feel free to reach out if you encounter further challenges."

With that, Jason left the room, leaving behind a mix of

intrigue and uncertainty.

"Was that really the president?" Silas asked after all the guards had left. "What does he mean that we will be in touch?"

"I'm not too sure, but I don't have a good feeling about it," Amelia responded, her tone reflecting a mix of concern and uncertainty.

Jesse nodded, his irritation steaming. "I don't like any of this." He leaned forward. "One thing's clear: there's a reason this restaurant is so empty, except for the cook and the waitress. But how did he know we would be here in the first place?"

The waitress brought out their food, and they fell into a contemplative silence. Their meal was a mix of flavors and thoughts. After finishing their lunch, the waitress approached their table and informed them that the president had covered their bill. He had expressed the hope that this gesture would establish good faith between them.

Silas and Amelia exchanged puzzled looks. Meanwhile, Jesse stood and stormed out of the restaurant. They exchanged a glance before expressing gratitude to the waitress and following him.

As they caught up with him, Amelia spoke first. "What's bothering you, Jesse?"

"*My* issue?" he snapped. "My issue is that the government is interested in what we're doing. Can't you see that? His visit and the meal weren't about congratulations."

Confusion crossed Silas's face. "But why would the government be interested in us? We're just a research lab trying to advance medicine."

His voice dropped to a hushed tone, laden with urgency. "Open your eyes, you two. We can *time travel*. Do you honestly think that every government agency, political power, and major corporation won't want a piece of that? His visit wasn't to celebrate our success; it was to celebrate his own success in reaching us *first*. Imagine the potential horrors that could be unleashed with the power we possess."

Jesse's words hung in the air, a stark reminder of the staggering implications of their achievement. As they continued walking, the reality of their situation took on a new layer of complexity.

Amid the whirlwind of thoughts and emotions, they walked in silence for a while. But not toward the car. Instead, they reached a nearby park, where they found an empty bench and settled down, each lost in their own contemplations.

After a moment, Silas spoke, breaking the silence. "You're right, Jesse. We can't ignore the potential dangers. But how do we navigate this?"

"There isn't much we can do right now," Jesse said, his tone reflecting a mixture of determination and pragmatism. "At the moment, our best course of action is to stay on the path we've laid out. We're scheduled for another test next week, and we need to be fully prepared for that. However, we need to stay vigilant and keep our ears open. We don't know when he'll show up again, but I have a feeling he'll return in a few weeks, likely with his so-called friends."

As his statement hung in the air, Silas and Amelia exchanged looks and then nodded. For the time being, that was indeed the most prudent approach they could take to navigate this uncertain path they had embarked upon.

As Jesse drove them back, Silas leaned back in his seat, contemplating the whirlwind of experiences that had unfolded. He turned to Amelia, who sat beside him. Her expression was a mix of weariness and concern.

"Are you going to be okay, Silas?" she asked.

He managed a small smile and nodded. "Yeah, I think so. It's just a lot to process, you know?"

She reached over and placed a reassuring hand on his arm. "We'll figure this out together."

The car pulled up to his apartment building which he was very glad to remember where he lived, and he stepped out, feeling the cool night air against his skin. He turned back to them with gratitude in his eyes. "Thanks, both of you. I'll see you tomorrow."

Jesse nodded. "Rest up, Silas. Tomorrow's a new day."

She offered a warm smile. "And don't hesitate to reach out if you need anything."

As he made his way to his apartment, he couldn't help but feel a mix of uncertainty and determination. The day's events had opened a world of possibilities, along with a host of challenges. But with his friends by his side, he knew they would face it together.

Despite the day's progression, the world still felt a bit off to him since his return from time travel. He stepped out of the elevator on the eighth floor, guided by muscle memory. He navigated his way to a familiar doormat adorned with what had once been a clever joke, now faded and coated in grime.

He reached into his pocket, retrieved his keys, and identified the one he needed by its blue dot. Inside, a sensation of home greeted him. His keys found their place in a small dish on a side table next to the entrance. With a sigh, he slipped off his shoes and padded across the floor.

Moving with a sense of familiarity, Silas approached a window in his living room and drew back the curtains, revealing the cityscape before him. The sun, now beginning its descent, cast a warm glow over the urban landscape. Long shadows stretched across the streets and buildings. In this quiet moment, he had a sense of connection to the world around him, a feeling of belonging that he had missed during his time away.

Deliberately avoiding any news broadcasts, he opted to turn on an older sitcom from his youth, a lighthearted camaraderie of fictional friends. Hours passed as his mind eased. Eventually, he took a long shower, washing away the feeling of not having been truly clean in weeks, and climbed into bed, turning the TV back to the sitcom. As he watched, the screen's gentle glow and the characters' familiar voices lulled him to sleep.

Still, his dreams were a tangled web of sensations and memories where the boundaries of reality and fiction blurred once more. His past, present, and turkey escapade converged into a bewildering symphony.

As he envisioned his friends' deaths, the incongruous laugh track clashed with the gravity of those moments, creating a disconcerting dissonance that echoed in his mind. An imaginary crowd's reactions were strangely synchronized with the laugh track. Then came visions of Amelia's face, her expressions like scenes from a drama. The crowd and Amelia's emotions weaved a distorted narrative that blurred the lines between a sitcom and his emotions.

The world then transformed. Instead of humans, he found himself surrounded by turkeys, each character in his dream-scape adopting the form of the very creature he had once inhabited. He navigated a world of gobbling turkeys, where his own presence as the sole human stood out in stark contrast. Yet in the dream's twisted logic, it somehow made a strange sort of sense.

As the sun's gentle rays filtered through the curtains, Silas gradually stirred. His dreams, a swirling tapestry of memories and emotions, lingered on the edges of his consciousness. The laugh track, once a source of comfort, now echoed in his mind like a distorted melody. A lingering disorientation.

With a soft sigh, he blinked and gazed at the ceiling, collecting himself. He then reached over to the nightstand and switched off the television, silencing the incessant laughter from the show he had on. Sitting up, he ran a hand through his tousled hair. He just couldn't shake the feeling that his experiences had rewired something within him, that the boundaries of his reality had blurred.

Sliding out of bed, he padded over to the window and drew the curtains back once more. Warm morning hues bathed the cityscape, offering a tangible connection to the world. With each breath, he found himself inching toward his sense of self, to the person he was becoming.

The Fourth Chapter: A President's Intrigue

Sitting in the back seat of a spacious, heavily armored SUV, Jason gazed at the bustling streets out the window. He observed people going about their routines—heading to and from lunch, collecting dry cleaning and laundry, and grabbing coffee. All the typical scenes of a workday in progress. Amid this urban rhythm, he mused over the various intertwining lives.

"Mr. President, were there any additional stops you wished to make?" his driver said, interrupting his reverie.

President King shifted his gaze from the window to the driver. "No. Take me to the airport. I'd prefer to return as swiftly as possible. There are matters I need to attend to."

With a nod, the driver guided the vehicle toward the airport. The engine softly hummed as they navigated the city streets.

The president leaned back in his seat, his mind preoccupied with the weight of responsibilities that awaited him. As the SUV moved through the city's bustling roads, he considered the past few days and the complex implications of the machine that now existed under his command.

Outside, the cityscape gradually shifted. Skyscrapers and office buildings gave way to open spaces and runways. The SUV maneuvered onto the airport grounds, a well-practiced route that showcased the driver's familiarity.

After the SUV pulled through a secure entrance and onto the tarmac, it followed the designated path toward the colossal airplane that Jason would use. Exiting the car, he was greeted by a small entourage of aides and security personnel. He conveyed brief instructions and received updates on various matters.

He then ascended the aircraft steps, his entourage in tow. He settled into a seat toward the rear. As the plane prepared for takeoff, his thoughts delved into contemplation. He pondered the time travel machine and its unprecedented power. A vast potential for political influence. To both incite and prevent conflicts.

Jason's fingers rhythmically tapped the armrest, his mind racing through an array of scenarios and strategies that had the potential to reshape history. The allure of improving his country's history and future held a strong appeal. Not only would it benefit the nation, but his name could be etched into the archives of history.

But to do so, he knew he needed to gain the trio's support or establish an allegiance of his own.

Lost in his thoughts, he nearly missed the flight attendant's approach with refreshments. He politely declined and leaned back in his seat once more.

As the plane took flight, Jason's introspection carried on. He pulled out his computer and delved into the latest reviews of himself. The percentage of positive reviews was steadily increasing, thanks in part to his actions against the cult. Still, certain news stations had magnified the impact, broadcasting exaggerated stories. The rest of the country grew fearful of this emerging cult, believing that they were targeting innocent research scientists striving to advance humanity.

This had been Jason's plan all along. Ever since the trio—Amelia, Jesse, and Silas—achieved time travel, he had operatives from his elite forces masquerade as cult members and initiate attacks. In the confusion and uncertainty, who would the citizens of this great nation be more likely to believe? President Jason King or a group who many perceive as merely a collection of fanatics?

"Would you like something to drink or eat, Mr. President?" the flight attendant inquired.

Startled, he looked up, just realizing she was standing before him. "Oh, you can call me Jason." He gave her a suave smile. "And yes, I would like a whiskey sour. Thank you."

Returning his smile, the attendant prepared the drink and handed him the glass. "Here you go, Jason." She gave him a playful wink and then moved away, her attention shifting to the rest of the entourage.

Taking a sip of his drink, Jason resumed his focus on his computer. He clicked a link on his desktop and opened a collection of camera footage, each labeled with descriptions. He selected "Silas Apartment Front Door." The footage expanded, showcasing Silas's brown apartment door. A short while later, a vehicle pulled up—a vehicle he recognized as belonging to Jesse Stein. Silas emerged from the vehicle and approached his apartment door. Shifting to a different camera, Jason traced Silas's path to the elevator and to his apartment.

With precision, Jason switched to another camera, which was situated inconspicuously on the fridge like a magnet. His focus remained unwavering as he watched Silas enter the apartment and flip through a notebook. Shifting his view to a camera hidden in the ceiling fan, he observed the notebook's detailed drawings and instructions. A sense of realization dawned on him. Within the pages were the blueprint for the time travel machine!

That notebook stood as the linchpin of Jason's success, particularly if the trio chose not to align with his intentions.

But Jason also recognized the gravity of the situation. Winning them over was no longer just a strategic move; it was a pressing necessity.

Maintaining vigilant surveillance over the three—particularly Silas—was paramount. That was why he took the initiative to "assist" them by augmenting security measures at the facility. He needed to know their moves and their thoughts to convince them. He needed to know *them*.

As he sat there, he conceived a multifaceted plan. The crux of it involved engineering a seeming attack on the facility, all while discreetly deploying his control team. The intricate orchestration carried its share of calculated risks—his own operatives' lives were on the line, as well as those of the facility's personnel. It was a high-stakes gambit, one that required a master manipulator.

The plan needed to be distressing enough to stir doubts and fears yet contained to avert actual harm. The line between danger and security had to be blurred, allowing him to step in as the savior they'd never expected.

Jason closed his laptop, secured it in his bag, and handed it over to one of his entourage members for safekeeping. Leaning back, he shut his eyes and allowed his thoughts to drift amid the events of the day and the intricate challenges that awaited him.

The rumbling of the plane's wheels contacting the tarmac roused him from his slumber. Bracing himself for the forward jolt, he observed the controlled deceleration as the aircraft navigated the tarmac. Within moments, his entourage and security personnel disembarked, leaving one individual behind. They signaled that the surroundings were secure, and he confidently exited the plane.

Due to the flight's unscheduled nature, the media was notably absent, sparing him from incessant inquiries and camera flashes. After he settled within his vehicle, his secretary provided him with a comprehensive rundown of the day's developments. He informed the secretary of his intent to engage with the Control captain, to address concerns. In reality, the discussion was a calculated maneuver, an opportunity to lay out his strategic plans.

They drove for approximately thirty minutes before arriving at the White House. At the rear of the property, they accessed a concealed garage that led into an underground parking area. They pulled up beside large steel doors, which were already open in anticipation of Jason's arrival, and parked the vehicles. The driver exited and opened the door for both Jason and his secretary.

"Welcome home, Mr. President," the driver said.

Jason nodded in acknowledgment, receiving his bag from an entourage member. He entered the building and traversed several hallways. During their walk, the secretary inquired if there was anything he needed before his meeting with the captain.

"Is the chef still on the premises?" he asked.

"No. I'm sorry. He left about an hour ago. His daughter is ill with the flu."

"No worries. I'm glad he could be there for his daughter. Please have someone arrange for a burger and fries, along with a large orange soda, from any open establishment."

With a nod, she promptly initiated the necessary arrangements.

Continuing to his office without her, Jason noted that the late hour had left the building sparsely populated. He exchanged acknowledgments with the few guards, janitors, and night-shift employees who were wrapping up their duties. The tranquility allowed him to gather his thoughts.

The doors swung open, guided by two guards, and revealed Joel Sanders, the captain of Control, standing by the president's desk. He was a broad-shouldered man with dark hair and deep brown eyes. He stood slightly taller than the president and was dressed in tan pants and a dark blue shirt—his uniform partially assembled.

He held a picture frame in his hand, his gaze fixed on it. "You truly have a beautiful family here, Jason. But who's the third child in this photo? I've always intended to ask, but the need only arises now, having been roused from sleep this late at night. "

Jason accepted the photo from him and studied it. "One day, she was gone—vanished when she was eighteen. We scoured everywhere, but we could never locate her. It's been about eight years since she left." He set the photo down on his desk and gestured to the two couches that faced each other.

Joel poured himself a glass of vodka over ice and settled onto the couch, positioned to face the door.

The president took a seat on the opposite couch. "I have a plan that needs to stay within the confines of this room, between you and me. And I need your assistance in reviewing and refining it."

Joel took a sip of his drink, his expression indicating approval.

The door swung open, and the secretary hurried into the room, holding a brown bag in one hand and a large orange soda in the other. "I apologize for the interruption, sir, but here's your food." She extended the bag toward Jason.

After expressing his gratitude, he dismissed her, allowing her to leave for the night. The door closed behind her.

Jason unpacked the greasy burger and fries, placing them on the table. He offered some of his fries to Joel, who politely declined, citing his aversion to fast food.

"More for me then," Jason replied with a grin. He proceeded to enjoy a few bites of his meal before delving into his plan to win over the facility and seize control of the time travel machine.

Joel listened and occasionally interjected to offer his opinions, which provided Jason with brief moments to take further bites of his food. Over an hour or two, they refined the plan, honing the details. Including the first step: sending an expedited letter to the research facility, informing them that Jason would be visiting in two weeks.

The president took a sip of his drink, his tone serious. "Remember, once this operation is underway, if any of your men are apprehended, it can't be traced back to us. We'll need to shift blame elsewhere."

Joel nodded knowingly. "Is there any other way to handle this?" he quipped, resulting in a shared chuckle.

The Fifth Chapter: Into the Unknown

The trio settled on traveling just twenty years ahead.

Amelia came up with the brilliant idea to bury capsules in Jesse's backyard now, only she aware of their contents. Jesse and Silas would remain oblivious, ensuring a test to validate its success. Silas would travel to the future, find the capsules, and come back. The plan hinged on Jesse being home the day Silas made the journey, anticipating the presence of someone to witness the culmination of their efforts.

Silas donned comfortable clothing and reclined on the medical bed, his mind racing with a mixture of anticipation and a touch of nervousness. Nearby, Jesse and Amelia were engrossed in reviewing last-minute notes, checking and rechecking the intricate mechanisms of the time travel machine.

Amelia gently wiped Silas's forearm and inserted a needle, the conduit for an IV drip that would keep him nourished throughout the taxing time travel experience. She then attached wires to his chest and connected them to monitors that would track his vital signs. Securing The Machine's wires to his head formed an intricate network that resembled a sweatband adorned with an array of wires. As she tended to him, Jesse worked to ensure his body's stability, strapping his legs and arms down to prevent any involuntary movements that could compromise the process.

A sense of camaraderie and purpose charged the atmosphere.

As Amelia secured the last wire and double-checked the readings on the monitors, she exchanged a glance with Jesse, a silent affirmation that they were ready to proceed.

"Silas, are you ready?" she asked, her voice a steady anchor amid the mounting anticipation.

He nodded. "As ready as I'll ever be."

Jesse stepped closer, offering a reassuring smile. "You've got this, Silas. We're right here with you every step of the way."

Silas closed his eyes, focusing on his breathing to steady his nerves. The room seemed to hold its breath as Amelia initiated the sequence, The Machine's hum gradually intensifying.

She and Jesse monitored the process, their expressions a blend of anticipation and concern. The Machine's whirring reached a crescendo before subsiding, the room returning to its previous stillness. The pulsating light faded, and the monitors displayed stable readings.

While Silas remained physically present, his consciousness seemed distant, almost as if he was in a deep slumber. They maintained a vigilant watch over the machines, ensuring every aspect was being tracked.

Amelia's brow furrowed. "Given his current state of being, what's our plan for the visit by the president and his captain in a few days? What if Silas does not wake up by then?"

Jesse glanced at Silas, his expression thoughtful. "We'll need to figure out how to manage both. It's crucial we don't compromise the integrity of either endeavor."

Amelia nodded, her mind already racing to find a solution. "Perhaps we can create a temporary containment protocol for

The Machine. We can explain that we're in the midst of a critical experiment that requires privacy and security."

His gaze focused on Silas's still form. "That could work. We'll have to ensure the president's visit doesn't disrupt our progress while keeping our breakthrough confidential."

As the two of them strategized, several hours elapsed, and Silas remained in his unconscious state. His vitals remained stable.

"I think it's a good idea if we take a break and have lunch," Amelia suggested. "Since he's still stable."

Jesse nodded and relayed his lunch order to her, who left to retrieve the food. When she returned with lunch, the two of them sat to eat, occasionally checking the monitors. Between bites of food, they discussed the experiment and the potential implications. Afterward, they cleaned up and resumed their positions, keeping a watchful eye on the machines and monitors.

As the sun began its descent, Jesse turned his gaze toward the window. With a contemplative expression, he shifted his attention to Amelia. "Let's let everyone go home early tonight. They deserve to spend time with their families and to unwind. They've truly earned it."

She nodded. "You head home as well. Spend some quality time with your wife and daughter. You've barely had the chance to be together over the past week due."

He attempted to argue the contrary, but she remained resolute in her insistence. A smile crept across his face. He wrapped up his remaining tasks, shared a heartfelt hug with Amelia, and departed.

Hours passed as Silas remained ever the same. Amelia paced, engrossed in reviewing charts and watching him. She didn't even notice the stars twinkling in the evening sky out the window.

After she retrieved a bag of BBQ chips from the break room, her phone chimed with a text message. It was a photo from Jesse, capturing his ten year old daughter in the midst of chasing butterflies.

A warm smile formed on her lips. "Very cute!" she responded. "She's getting so big!"

A loud crash shattered the air, originating from Silas's room.

Amelia's grip on the bag of chips faltered, causing it to slip from her hand. She sprinted toward the commotion. Turning into the room, she found Silas still in his bed—but surrounded by shattered glass.

A faint breeze rustled the air, and she turned and noticed a broken window. On the floor lay a brick with a note attached.

Cautiously maneuvering through the broken glass, she reached the brick and carefully detached the note. She read the message.

"Go to Hell, you science freaks!"

A sigh escaped her lips as she set the brick and note down on a nearby table. She captured an image of them and sent it to Jesse, along with a text:

"We're okay here. Those individuals are unruly. Contacting security to involve the police."

She took a moment to assess the damage and ensure Silas's well-being. He appeared unharmed. She quickly notified the security team, requesting their immediate presence to secure the area and assess any potential threats.

Within minutes, security personnel arrived, followed shortly by Jesse, who had rushed back to the facility.

"Are you okay?" he asked as he entered the room, concern

etched across his face. "What happened?"

She nodded, her voice steady despite the tension. "I'm fine. I was in the hallway when I heard the crash. Someone threw a brick with a threatening note through the window."

His expression darkened as he examined the shattered window and the debris around it. "This is getting out of hand," he muttered. Taking a deep breath, he turned his attention back to her. "Let's make sure Silas is secure. Then we'll work with security to review the footage and identify whoever did this."

They checked Silas's connections and ensured that the time travel process hadn't been compromised. As they did so, security personnel examined the note, the brick, and the window, looking for any clues that could lead to the culprit's identity.

The minutes ticked by, the room abuzz with activity. Jesse's phone buzzed with a response from the police, who had been alerted by the security team. They confirmed that officers were on their way to investigate the incident further.

Amid the chaos, Amelia's attention shifted to Silas, who was now stirring. "Jesse! Silas is awake!" She approached the medical bed.

"Everyone out!" Jesse ordered. "We'll call you back in a little bit."

His command was met with swift compliance as everyone exited the room without any resistance.

He turned his focus back to Silas, relief and excitement mingling in his expression. He reviewed the monitors and verified that everything appeared to be in order. "How are you feeling, Silas?"

The restraints that held Silas in place were undone, allowing him to wipe residue away from his eyes. His vision had improved, enabling him to see everyone more clearly.

His voice resonated with emotion. "Your father's watch and the note I wrote you during our first year in college."

A smile graced Amelia's lips, her eyes shining. "He did it, Jesse! He was really there! That's amazing!"

In that moment of triumph, the challenges and doubts that had surrounded their ambitious endeavor seemed to melt away. Their tangible success created hope. As they basked in this breakthrough, they remembered the remarkable journey they had undertaken—a journey that now held the potential to reshape their understanding of time and space.

Silas's gaze shifted to the broken window and the brick. His expression grew somber. He motioned toward the brick. "But we can't ignore those who are willing to go to such lengths to halt our progress."

Amelia nodded, resolve flickering in her eyes. "You're right, Silas. We can't let these threats deter us. If anything, it shows that what we're doing has the potential to disrupt those who fear change."

"We'll need to take precautions," Jesse added with a firm tone. "Increase security and be vigilant."

Silas nodded. "Agreed. We've come too far to let this setback stop us. Let's make sure we're prepared for whatever comes next."

The trio set to work, not just to protect their breakthrough but to ensure that their journey into the future continued undeterred.

"I suppose this will play into the president's idea of bolstering security with his personal team here," Jesse remarked, his words laced with concern. "But I hope it doesn't lead him to think we need more surveillance."

"If he wasn't keeping an eye on us at all times before, he most definitely will be now," Silas said.

They all nodded.

"Hey, Jesse. Would you mind grabbing me something to drink and snack on? That really took a toll on me."

Jesse nodded, offering him a reassuring pat on the shoulder before heading out.

Left alone, Amelia turned her attention to him. "What was that all about?" she asked, her expression a mix of curiosity and worry.

Silas let out a heavy sigh and met her gaze. "The future was drastically different. Not flying cars or living on another planet different, but there was rampant violence—burning cars and broken buildings. People were resorting to theft and robbery, desperate for anything they could get their hands on. And the president—well, his *captain*—was at the helm of it. A curfew was imposed at six p.m. daily. The military was under his thumb; the president had granted him full control."

A somber silence settled.

"It wasn't confined to the US; it was a global upheaval. He somehow had sway over everything, staying one step ahead. I can't explain how, but he had foresight and control. It took me an entire week to travel a mere fifteen miles to Jesse's house…"

Her expression turned grave as she comprehended the implications. "And Jesse?"

"He was…gone." Silas's voice wavered. "So was his wife. Their daughter was barely surviving amid a crumbling home. Frequent power outages. Every twenty minutes. Thankfully, Jesse had informed her of my return. She was there waiting, shovel in hand. I unearthed what I needed. Afterward, I knew I had to return to all of you. I cut myself and let myself bleed out, just as we'd predicted to do. Reaching a state of unconsciousness allowed me to awaken back here."

She placed a comforting hand on his arm. "I can't imagine what you just went through, Silas. To witness such a nightmarish future…"

Silas's voice cracked. "I…I can't stand by and let that reality become our fate. We can't go down that path." He paused, trying to find his words. "Wha…what do we tell Jesse?"

She looked down, deep in thought. "I…I don't know. If we tell him, it could alter the events, but then again, if his fate is to die, wouldn't it happen one way or another?"

He was equally uncertain. "Perhaps we should withhold that part until we gather more information."

Amelia nodded. "That might be the best approach for now. We need to be cautious."

Jesse reentered the room with a bag of chips and a drink and with concern evident in his eyes. "Everything all right?"

She exchanged a glance with Silas. "Silas had a rough experience during the time travel."

His expression softened. "I can't even imagine. Silas, if you need anything, just let me know."

Silas managed a small smile. "Thanks."

Silas recounted what he had experienced, carefully omitting the part about Jesse's and his wife's fates. Only mentioned that he hadn't seen them. Jesse's expression shifted as a sense of unease settled over him.

They then sat in contemplative silence. Ultimately, they decided sleep would provide them with a fresh perspective in the morning.

Jesse summoned the security team and cleaning crew to

address the broken window. After a temporary plywood fix was in place, they made their way out of the facility.

Amelia offered to drive Silas home, and Jesse bid them both a goodnight. During the drive, silence accompanied them until she broke it.

"Were you able to find a glimpse of our futures?"

Silas, still processing his memories, looked out the window. "No. I couldn't find any trace of us. Jesse's daughter mentioned that she hadn't seen us for a long time."

They continued the drive without much conversation, the music providing a soothing backdrop. Eventually, they arrived at Silas's apartment.

"Would you mind coming up?" he asked, still sitting in the car. "It's just so quiet in my apartment. We could watch a movie or something."

She agreed, and they both made their way upstairs.

Once inside, he offered wine, which she gladly accepted after the chaotic week. He poured them each a glass, and they shared a moment of laughter. Sitting on his bed, they opted for a lighthearted romantic comedy from their college days, his arm draped around her.

The wine bottle eventually emptied, leaving them both with a pleasant buzz. A level of comfort he hadn't experienced in a long time graced him. He planted a gentle kiss on her forehead, and she responded by wrapping her arms around his torso. In a matter of minutes, tranquility lulled them into a peaceful slumber.

The Sixth Chapter: The Presidential Arrival

The president's plane arrived at the terminal, and Jason and Joel disembarked before getting into the designated vehicles that would transport them to the research facility.

As the vehicles navigated toward the facility, Jason reviewed his plans with Joel. He anticipated gaining more insight into the machine's function, seeking valuable information that might prove crucial if his efforts to win the researchers over failed.

"Are you confident about the plan?" Joel inquired, breaking the silence.

He paused, considering his response. The uncertainty of the situation *did* weigh heavily on his mind. "I am extremely confident in this approach. Our best bet is to appear cooperative, build trust, and address their concerns. Hopefully, by meeting them halfway, we can achieve our goals."

The vehicles reached the facility's entrance, and Jason's focus zeroed in on the intricate meeting that lay ahead. He stepped out of the vehicle, ready to put their strategy into motion.

Standing by the entrance, Amelia, Jesse, and Silas observed the presidential vehicles pulling up.

"Let's act as though it's just a regular day," she suggested.

"Share enough information without being overly specific. Show respect and maintain a pleasant demeanor."

Jesse and Silas nodded.

As the president and his captain alighted from the vehicle, they approached the entrance, where Amelia, Jesse, and Silas were still waiting.

"It's a pleasure to see you three again," the president said. "Hopefully, we're all feeling a bit more at ease now that we're on your home ground. Allow me to introduce Captain Joel, the head of my control team. His team is responsible for employing the security personnel here, and he'll be augmenting their numbers to provide additional protection against those cultists."

With smiles exchanged, a moment of silence hung in the air.

"Well then, shall we begin the tour?" Jesse suggested, which was met with unanimous agreement.

This particular machine they showed, although smaller in size compared to Silas's version, had yielded positive results. Jesse explained how they had fine-tuned the technology and addressed any issues to ensure its safety and functionality. Amelia chimed in, elaborating on the complex algorithms they had developed to regulate the process and prevent any undesirable outcomes.

The president and Captain Joel listened, occasionally interjecting with questions that demonstrated genuine interest. Silas stayed back and observed their reactions, sensing an opportunity to foster understanding and cooperation.

After the tour, they moved to the control room, where Silas discussed the monitoring and control mechanisms they had implemented to oversee the time travel process. The president and his captain appeared impressed by the operation.

However, the president also noticed the notebook from Silas's apartment that he had seen on his computer. He made sure not to linger too long on it with his eyes.

They then gathered in a meeting room, a modest space furnished with a table and a few chairs, to discuss further details. Silas, Jesse, and Amelia shared their findings, advancements, and potential applications. The president acknowledged the significance of their work and expressed his interest in supporting their endeavors.

Over the course of the conversation, Jason King's initial apprehensions eased. He saw the potential benefits this technology could offer, not only for their organization but for the nation. Silas's warnings from the future lingered in his mind, but he decided to put his trust in the present moment and the possibilities that lay ahead.

"Can we see the machine that you use?" Jason asked. "I would love to see it in person. This tour has been fantastic and all, but witnessing the machine would be the cherry on top."

Silas exchanged a quick glance with Jesse and Amelia, who nodded. "Of course, Mr. President. We can show you. Follow us." He led the way out of the control room.

As they exited, Captain Joel inquired, "Is there a bathroom nearby? I hate to ask, but all the water I had on my way over here has just gone right through me."

"Of course, Captain Joel," Amelia said with a smile. "Just down the hall and to your right. You can't miss it. We'll be just two doors down."

As he walked toward the restroom, he noticed the others enter another room. A sense of urgency gripped him, prompting him to return to the control room. There, he swiftly pulled out his phone and took pictures of the control room and the notebook. He then made his way back to everyone else.

He maintained his composure, pretending to wipe his hands as if he had just come from the restroom. The group welcomed him back without a second thought.

Silas, Jesse, and Amelia carried on with their explanation. Yet Jesse couldn't help but feel a subtle sense of suspicion creeping in. He couldn't quite shake the feeling that Captain Joel's bathroom break had been oddly timed. It was something he would need to discuss with the other two later.

"Is there any way we could get a demonstration?" the president asked. "Would it be possible, perhaps, for me to try this out? Purely out of curiosity."

The three looked at each other.

"We would love to show you how it works, Mr. President," Jesse said, "but we just used it the other day, and it's something that we must plan a few days in advance to ensure everything is in order. Otherwise, it might not work properly. There could be some unexpected issues if we attempt it on a whim." The response was not entirely untrue but certainly stretched the truth.

The president nodded. "I appreciate your thoroughness. Perhaps we can arrange for a future demonstration, properly scheduled when everything is in order."

The president then expressed his interest in discussing security measures with Captain Joel and his team. They guided the group back to the meeting room. The president took his seat, and the others followed suit.

"I'm considering sending more of Captain Joel's team to bolster your security here," the president said and addressed the recent brick incident. He found humor in the absurdity of wasting a good brick and chuckled. "Ultimately, the decision lies with Captain Joel, but I believe having additional personnel both outside and inside the building would be prudent. What do you think, Joel?"

Captain Joel nodded. "I concur, sir. Given their track record of attacking similar facilities and the potential threat they pose, I believe it's in your best interest to have as much protection as possible. Especially if they learn of your success, there's no telling what they might do."

Silas, Jesse, and Amelia exchanged glances.

"Sir, it's very thoughtful of you to take this step," she said. "However, we have to wonder if these individuals would truly want to harm any of us. What purpose would it serve other than hindering their own cause?"

"Unfortunately, belief can drive people to commit heinous acts," Captain Joel responded firmly, "even if it seems counter-intuitive. They view what you're doing as a direct challenge to their beliefs, and that can lead to extreme actions."

Amelia considered this. "In that case, we appreciate your offer and will accept the added security measures."

"I also think we should have members of Control accompany you when you're outside of this facility for protection. They won't interfere with your daily activities, and you may not even notice their presence, but it's for your safety. Having them stationed outside your homes would be a prudent measure as well."

This proposal intensified Silas's, Amelia's, and Jesse's concerns about the increasing level of intrusion. Now, they would be under the president's constant watch.

The president nodded. "Excellent. We'll make sure your safety is our top priority. Captain Joel, please arrange for the necessary personnel and security measures."

Captain Joel gave a firm nod. "Understood, Mr. President. I'll have our team ensure the facility is well-protected."

With the security matter settled, the discussion turned to other topics. They talked about the time travel technology's potential benefits and how it could impact various fields, from science to history.

As their meeting continued, Silas, Jesse, and Amelia couldn't help but wonder about the president's true intentions. Nevertheless, they played their part, sharing their knowledge and expertise while guarding their secrets carefully.

The president's visit concluded with a sense of cautious optimism. They bid their farewells, and President King and Captain Joel returned to their vehicles, taking their seats in the back of one. The vehicles then drove away.

"Did you obtain what we required?" the president inquired.

"Yes," the captain replied. "I managed to capture images of every page in the notebook."

"Excellent. We will have them printed and sent to the team we rescued from the so-called cult attack. Let's see what they can glean from this. I don't believe we completely won them over today, but now we will have ears everywhere."

The Seventh Chapter: Invasive Visitors

Over the next week following the presidential visit, Amelia, Jesse, and Silas continued their work as normal—well, as normal as possible—with all the new security members. These individuals didn't seem to blend in with the other guards. They were much bigger than their average athletic-type guard, carrying guns and wearing bulky body armor. Their color schemes consisted of blue and black, and while some wore helmets, those were mainly used outside. The ones inside wore masks that covered most of their faces.

For the most part, they didn't get in the way. The only instances where the three saw them do more than their usual rounds were the few times when the protesters became excessively rowdy and loud. On those occasions, they resorted to using pepper spray, which Silas, Jesse, and Amelia believed was the *wrong* way to handle the situation, but they couldn't do anything about it.

Despite the discomfort and unease that came with the heightened security, Silas, Jesse, and Amelia managed to maintain their focus. They delved deeper into their research, driven by their desire to make time travel technology safer and more reliable.

Amid all the chaos, they made significant progress. They developed a method for more precise selection of the host bodies they inhabited, ensuring they didn't inadvertently harm the individuals they temporarily displaced. Additionally, they cracked the code for a return mechanism that eliminated the need to go unconscious due to blood loss.

Instead of having Silas undergo the travel, they conducted interviews to find suitable individuals for future jumps. However, they hadn't had much success with identifying the right candidate so far.

As they worked diligently, the weight of their discoveries and the responsibility they bore weighed on their shoulders. Each breakthrough brought them one step closer, but it also heightened their sense of urgency. With Control monitoring their every move, they knew they had to proceed with caution.

Outside their research, they couldn't help but notice the growing tension in the world. The cultist activities seemed to be escalating with more frequent protests and acts of violence.

"What if we're inadvertently feeding into the cultists' fears and anger?" Amelia asked one evening. "Our research and experiments are pushing the boundaries of what's considered ethical and safe. Could they see us as the real threat?"

Silas nodded. "It's a valid point. We need to prepare for the possibility that our actions might not only attract the attention of Control but also further provoke those who oppose our work."

"Perhaps we should consider reaching out to other scientists or organizations who share our vision for responsible time travel," Jesse said. "Collaboration might help legitimize our efforts and ease the concerns of those who fear the unknown."

"And if we can demonstrate the positive impact of time travel, it might change public perception," she added.

With these thoughts in mind, they continued their work, determined to navigate the delicate balance between scientific progress, ethical responsibility, and the ever-watchful eyes of Control and the world beyond.

The day ended, and they collectively decided it was time to call it a day. But as they wrapped up their research, they couldn't help but notice the increasing intensity of the commotion outside. Shouts and screams reverberated through the air.

Amelia glanced out of the window, which had been fixed following the president's visit. She dismissed the scene as a typical protest with its shouting and picket signs, so she returned to her desk. However, a few minutes later, the unmistakable sound of gunfire shattered. All three of them froze and exchanged anxious glances.

"Could we be under attack like the other facilities?" Amelia asked.

"I believe so, but let's stay away from the windows," Jesse said. "Control can handle this situation, but we must exercise caution."

The uproar outside gradually subsided. The shooter or shooters seemed to have either fled, been apprehended, or subdued by force. But just as the trio relaxed, a deafening explosion rocked the room. The window shattered, and the trio was thrown to the ground.

Silas, dazed but uninjured, slowly regained his composure. His ears rang, but there was no sign of blood. He looked around and saw Jesse and Amelia were also getting to their feet, seemingly unharmed.

They attempted to communicate, but it became apparent

that none of them could hear. A Control member entered the room and gestured for them to follow. As they followed him, Silas's hearing returned, though muffled by the continuous gunfire and screams in the background.

They reached the end of the hallway, where the entrance lay in turmoil. People pounded on the glass doors, attempting to force their way inside. Control officers inside brandished firearms. The glass, already weakened from the explosion, succumbed to the relentless assault, allowing at least fifteen individuals to surge in.

The trio's guide from Control managed to snap them out of their stunned state, and they ran once more, heading toward the break room, which had an exit. Along the way, they passed numerous rooms filled with frightened people. As they passed the entrance to the parking garage, they were met with a terrifying sight—the garage was ablaze.

Flames cast eerie, dancing shadows across their path. Smoke seeped into the hallway, and the acrid scent stung their nostrils.

The situation was spiraling into chaos faster than they could comprehend.

With no other options, they rushed back and headed into the dimly lit break room, slamming the door behind them. Silence persisted, a stark contrast to the pandemonium just outside. Silas, Jesse, and Amelia exchanged worried looks, trying to communicate through frantic gestures.

The Control officer scribbled onto a piece of paper. "Stay here. I'll try to get back up." He then slipped out of the room, closing the door behind him.

The trio stood there, anxiety gnawing at them as they watched the door. Eventually, they sat against the wall opposite to the door, their minds consumed by thoughts of their families and the horrifying scenes they'd witnessed.

Outside, the chaos escalated even more. Gunfire and shouts filled the air.

Minutes felt like hours. The air grew heavy. They couldn't help but wonder about the fate of their research, their facility, and the figures responsible for this mayhem.

The Control member returned twenty-five minutes later. "We have everything under control for now, but it's not safe for you. Let's go!"

They all rose to their feet and followed the officer to the exit door in the break room.

He opened it cautiously, peering outside before swinging it wide. "Stay close behind," he instructed, and they nodded.

They followed him through the courtyard at a brisk pace. Three cars pulled up. The officer opened the door of the middle vehicle, and the trio piled in. After he slammed the door, the vehicles sped away from the chaos.

The ride remained tense, each passing moment only intensifying the gravity of what had just occurred. Silas, Amelia, and Jesse exchanged worried looks but said nothing.

As the chaos faded into the distance, the grim officer who drove with a clenched jaw finally broke the silence. "You three are safe now," he said. "We'll take you somewhere secure."

"Where are we going?" Jesse asked, his voice trembling.

The officer glanced at them in the rearview mirror. "I'm taking you all home. We will have officers outside your respective homes to make sure nothing bad happens."

The three exchanged looks once more.

"I would like to be dropped off at Silas's house and not mine," Amelia said. "I don't want to be alone."

The driver considered the request for a moment and then

looked forward. "That'll be fine. I will still put people outside your home to make sure nothing goes wrong." He then radioed in the plan.

As they drove, a heavy silence hung in the vehicle. The reality of the attack left them all vulnerable and exposed. The once-familiar streets now felt eerie, their homes looming as both a comfort and a reminder of the day's unsettling events.

Upon arriving at Silas's house, they saw the reassuring presence of two Control officers stationed outside. Silas and Amelia stepped out of the vehicle and thanked the driver for his assistance.

Inside, the atmosphere was somber. They couldn't help but replay the attack in their minds.

Amelia, sitting on his couch, broke the silence. "What's happening to our world? It's spiraling into chaos."

"We can't ignore what we've seen," he said. "But we also can't lose sight of our mission."

"Yeah… We can't let fear paralyze us."

Silas walked over to a kitchen cabinet and retrieved a bottle of vodka and two glasses. He poured them both a very generous shot and brought all three items with him over to the couch. "Drink this."

They both took a swig. The smooth liquid burned at first, but after a few seconds, it warmed them inside. They took another swig and relaxed a bit more, just staring at each other for a while.

Silas poured a third vodka shot.

Afterward, he turned on the shower, undressed her with care, and led her into the shower's warmth. He undressed as well. The warm water felt amazing on their skin.

Silas washed her body gently with nothing but care. She

smiled for the first time since the attack, turned around, and kissed his lips and forehead. Gently grabbing his shoulders, she brought him under the water, cleaning his body as he did hers. Afterward, they just held each other, their bond stronger than most.

They found solace in each other's arms.

Silas leaned in, and their lips met in a passionate embrace. It was as if the universe had conspired to bring them this moment of respite, reminding them that amid the turmoil, there could be moments of tenderness.

After the shower, they wrapped themselves in plush towels and returned to the living room. Silas poured another round of vodka. They sat on the couch, close but not speaking. Content in each other's presence. The day's events still lingered in their minds, but for now, they found comfort in each other.

After a few minutes, Amelia rested her head on his shoulder. He kissed the top of her head before deciding to move. He gently lifted her, taking the bottle of vodka with him, and carried her to his bedroom, where they both settled in close. He wrapped his arm around her and put on their favorite movie. Laughter filled the room, providing a much-needed respite from the day's events.

"Are you hungry?" he asked with a smile.

She chuckled. "I can always eat."

He grabbed his phone and ordered pizza. "After today, we need something greasy and unhealthy." He then called one of the guards outside to inform them about the order.

As they waited for the pizza to arrive, Silas and Amelia watched the movie.

She turned to him with a soft smile. "You know, no matter what happens, we'll always find a way to make it through together."

He nodded, his eyes filled with gratitude. He couldn't help but think about how lucky he was to have her by his side. "I don't know what I would do without you, Amelia."

The doorbell interrupted their moment of intimacy. The pizza. They devoured the pizza, indulging in its comforting taste. As the evening wore on, both satiated and a bit tipsy, they lay there wrapped in their towels, the movie credits rolling on the screen.

Amelia, her head resting on his chest, spoke. "What now?"

Silas, with a playful glint in his eye, grinned. "I have an idea."

He, thinking he got out of bed gracefully, stumbled into the kitchen. He grabbed some cookies and then fetched two spoons and a pint of cookie dough ice cream from the freezer. With a big smile, he returned to the room.

She laughed. "That's not what I was expecting, but it looks amazing!" She snatched the ice cream and spoon out of his hand, ripped open the top of the pint, and dove in.

They sat there, enjoying the little things. Silas looked over and noticed that she had chocolate on her cheek and some ice cream on the side of her mouth. He laughed and wiped it off with his finger. He then leaned in and kissed her.

The soft touch of his lips on hers was just what she needed. He leaned back, and she opened her eyes, smiled, and scooted closer to him. They proceeded to eat their junk food and finish off the bottle of vodka.

"I don't know if I can sleep tonight," she admitted. "I'm afraid I'll just relive it all over again."

"Well, we can lie here all night with our eyes glued open, and if you happen to fall asleep, I'll be here to make sure nothing happens."

She smiled. "Let's watch some cartoons to lighten the mood."

So, they proceeded to watch a popular adult cartoon. At some point, exhaustion overtook them. He noticed her eyes growing heavy and her head drooping onto his shoulder. He smiled, knowing she had found a moment of respite.

He gently leaned over, kissed her forehead, and whispered, "It's okay. I'll be right here with you."

She nodded and let her eyelids fall, finding comfort in his presence. Soon, they both drifted off to sleep, still wrapped in their towels and with the cartoon softly playing in the background.

Loud banging on the door startled them awake.

Silas sat up quickly and checked the clock. It read 5:29 a.m. He cautiously made his way to the door and peeped through the peephole to find one of the Control officers standing outside.

He opened the door. "Yes? Can I help you?"

"Captain Joel said that he has a team investigating what happened yesterday," the guard replied. "He asked you three to not come in today. To recover from yesterday and to stay away from the building while they conduct their investigation. We will keep you informed with any updates."

Silas watched as the guard walked away, his heavy footsteps echoing down the hallway. He closed the door, a bit confused, returned to the bedroom, and shared the message with Amelia.

Her brow furrowed. "It's strange, isn't it? I mean, why wouldn't they want the police to investigate?"

He nodded, his mind racing with questions. "I'm not sure, but it does seem odd. Maybe Captain Joel has his reasons, but it just feels...off."

As they contemplated their next steps, Silas couldn't shake the feeling that something much bigger was at play, something beyond the recent attack.

After sitting on the bed for about an hour, with the aftermath of their junk food binge surrounding them, Amelia asked, "How does breakfast sound?"

He glanced at the remnants of their indulgence—a pizza box, an empty ice cream tub, an empty vodka bottle, and a cookie tray—and chuckled. "Can we get something that isn't completely junk food?"

They both laughed, and she agreed.

Silas got up, gathered the trash, and disposed of it in the kitchen trash can. Returning to his room, he found she had stripped the bed for washing as they were covered in melted ice cream, crumbs, and spilled vodka. They soon showered together once more, mixing in plenty of kisses.

Under the warm, soothing water, they lost track of time. Their laughter echoed in the small bathroom as they playfully splashed water at each other. Eventually, their bodies pressed against each other. They kissed each other as the water flowed down their bodies. Soon, their kisses deepened, their hands explored, and they lost themselves in the heat of the moment, momentarily forgetting the chaos of the world outside.

After a while, they reluctantly stepped out of the shower. Silas wrapped a towel around his waist and handed one to her. As she dried herself off, he couldn't help but smile, appreciating the way the world seemed a little less daunting when they were together.

Amelia, her eyes filled with a mixture of desire and gratitude, pulled him into a tender kiss. "Thank you for being here," she muttered.

He kissed her forehead. "Always, Amelia. Always."

He offered her some of his clothes, and after finding a

comfortable outfit, she gave him a playful twirl.

"How do I look?" she asked with a grin.

He couldn't help but smile. "You look amazing, as always."

With a quick kiss, they left the bathroom. He called the guard, asking if it was okay for them to go to breakfast. The guard informed him that they could take his car, but someone from security would follow them. Silas, though not showing it, reluctantly agreed to the terms.

Before they left, something caught Silas's eye on the coffee table. He then thought of his notebook, which contained all their research and information. Which was just sitting there at their workplace.

Concerned, he turned to Amelia. "Should we be worried about any of our research getting out, Amelia?"

"I didn't think about that," she replied. "Maybe we should call Jesse and see what he thinks. Do you think he has any ideas about how to secure our research?"

Silas considered the early hour. "I'm sure he'll have some insights. But it's still quite early. Barely 7:30. He might not be up yet. We can ask him after breakfast. That way, if there is any concern, maybe we can sneak over and retrieve what we can."

He grabbed his car keys and their security badges—just in case.

The Eighth Chapter Secrets in Shadows

Sitting at his desk, the president received a call from Captain Joel, informing him that the plan will activate in one hour. The president summoned his secretary and instructed her to clear the rest of his day. If anyone questioned it, she was to explain that a situation that involved his daughters had arisen. She looked puzzled but complied.

He then called his wife and explained that he might not be able to make it to dinner due to an unexpected development with Captain Joel. She sounded irritated but understood that his duties took precedence.

Afterward, he placed an order with the kitchen for a chicken cordon bleu and mashed potatoes, along with two colas in glass bottles with real sugar. They assured him it would be delivered in thirty minutes. He hung up and turned his attention back to his computer.

Exactly thirty-one minutes later, a member of the kitchen staff brought his meal and set it on his desk. He thanked them, and they exited, closing the door behind them.

As the hour drew near, he pulled up the facility's camera footage on the television screen to have a comprehensive view and monitored the radio chatter. With his fork and knife in hand, he ate his meal and took a gulp of his cold beverage.

"Five minutes, everyone," Captain Joel said over the radio.

He continued to eat while gunshots rang out on camera one. Someone fired into the air, and Control swiftly neutralized the individual, kicking the gun away and securing them with zip ties. An explosion followed on camera two, and flames and smoke obscured the view. A satisfied smile crossed his face as he took another sip of his drink.

"Ross, go get the three and make sure they go by the entrance," Captain Joel ordered.

"Yes, sir."

The president switched to camera four and observed the three on the floor. Officer Ross escorted them out of the room, and the president followed them through various cameras. They arrived at the entrance just in time to witness the building being breached by the "mob," who was taken down one by one. The horror on their faces brought the president a twisted sense of satisfaction.

Jason couldn't help but revel in the power he wielded. The scenes on the screens were like a thrilling movie to him. He took another sip of his drink, feeling a rush of adrenaline.

The president's sinister satisfaction grew as he watched the trio move through the facility, their expressions a mixture of fear and confusion. The chaos outside had abated, but Control continued to maintain the illusion.

The president finished his cola, savoring the taste of victory, as Officer Ross led the trio out to the car. A few moments later, his phone rang, displaying Captain Joel's name on the screen. With a smirk, he answered.

"What do you think? How did we do?"

The president's response dripped with satisfaction. "Perfect.

I couldn't have done it better myself. Now, see what you can find with the team from the other facility. Let the three know you're investigating what happened but tell them tomorrow. Let's give them the night." He chuckled darkly. "We don't want to overwhelm them."

The president hung up and sat there, reflecting on the team's efficiency. Everything had unfolded just as he had planned. This operation would further cement his control over Silas, Jesse, and Amelia, rendering them *more* reliant on him and his protection. Giving him the upper hand.

The president closed his laptop and got up from his desk, eventually making his way out of the office. On his way, he sent a text to his secretary, telling her to finish up and go home and wishing her a good night. She replied with a thumbs-up emoji. He continued to the presidential housing side, where he found his two daughters watching a movie about a princess. He quietly walked in, gave his wife a big kiss, and then proceeded to kiss his daughters on the tops of their heads. Sitting next to his wife, he put his arm around her, and she rested her head on him.

"How was work?" she whispered to not to disturb the movie for the girls.

"Just a bunch of meetings that honestly could have all been handled through email," he replied, and they shared a light laugh.

As the movie progressed, the president's thoughts drifted back to the day's events. He couldn't help but feel a sense of satisfaction with how smoothly the operation had gone. He knew that the events had likely left the trio shaken and vulnerable, which was exactly where he wanted them.

It brought him a sense of power.

His wife sensed his contemplation and gently squeezed his hand. "Something on your mind, dear?" she asked, her voice barely audible over the movie.

He leaned down and kissed her forehead. "Just thinking about work," he replied with a reassuring smile. "But right now, I'd rather focus on our family and this movie. It's been a long day."

His wife nodded, and they both turned their attention back to the movie, cherishing the moments of tranquility.

The movie came to an end, filled with singing and a happy conclusion. The girls had fallen asleep, and he and his wife exchanged smiles. Without a word, they carried them to their beds. They took turns kissing their foreheads and leaving the doors slightly ajar.

As they made their way to their own bedroom, Jason wrapped his arms around his wife and planted a tender kiss on her neck. She turned around, meeting his kiss with a warm smile. He took out his phone and played some slow-dancing music. They held each other close, swaying to the music. Eventually, they made their way to bed and drifted off to sleep, finding comfort in each other.

As the sun streamed through the curtains, Jason found himself awake before his wife and daughters. He slowly got out of bed, donned some presidential sweats, and left the room. At his office, he called Joel.

"Good morning, Joel. Remember to send someone to their homes to let them know that they should take the day off. That we're conducting an investigation into this incident."

"Yes, sir. I'll keep you updated on what we find," Joel responded. "The team from the Boston facility will arrive in about an hour, and we'll have them assess the situation. We've already cleaned up the bodies, blood, and glass. I'll call you at noon with an update."

He thanked him and hung up.

Filled with pride, Jason decided to go for a jog. After finishing his workout in the downstairs gym, he wiped down the equipment and headed back to his family, which was when his wife started waking up.

"Good morning, sweetheart," he said, leaning over to kiss her. "How about we take the girls to get some donuts and then head to the park?"

"That sounds wonderful, honey, but please go shower first. You reek," she replied, laughing.

He sniffed his armpits and grimaced. "Yeah. That's probably smart."

After getting ready, the four of them made their way to their favorite local donut shop. The place had been called ahead of time to let them know that the president would be visiting with his family, so Secret Service agents would be there to ensure their safety. On the way there, their driver informed the president that the park would be cleared for them when they were ready to go.

They blissfully got donuts from the donut shop, where their girls were called little presidents. Jason handed the owner three hundred dollars, citing that he hoped it would help cover some of the lost earnings. The owner tried to refuse, but he wouldn't let him argue the matter.

They then made the short drive to the park. Upon arrival, Secret Service had already secured a spot at the park's playground for the family. The sun shined, and a gentle breeze rustled the leaves as they sat on a bench and enjoyed their donuts.

After their meal, Jason and Sarah watched with joy as their daughters ran around the playground, their laughter echoing. The park was practically empty, as word had spread that the president and his family were there. The few families who were present respected their privacy.

A few hours of swings, slides, and climbing structures later, it was getting close to noon and Joel's call. Sarah called someone in the kitchen to prepare a picnic, while he and Joel discussed the latest developments. He urged Joel to delay their return, if possible, and ensure copies of their research.

Afterward, Jason put the complexities of his work aside to focus on enjoying the day with his family. Today, he was simply a husband and father, making precious memories with his loved ones.

He joined Sarah and the girls, who were playing in the sand. Soon, a staff member from the kitchen arrived, and they enjoyed a lovely picnic with a basket of food. The joyful day continued with a game of frisbee and a leisurely walk.

As the sun dipped lower in the sky, they headed home. Jason and Sarah tucked their girls into bed before walking down the hall to their own room.

She hugged him gently. "You really needed this, Jason," she said softly. "We all did."

He nodded, having a deep sense of gratitude for the day. "Yes, we did. This presidency has been rough—not just on me but on all of us. I'm glad we had this time together."

"And the night isn't over yet; it's still early. How about we take a relaxing shower, put on some comfy clothes, grab some popcorn and candy, and head to the game room to watch a movie?"

His smile grew wider. "That sounds wonderful."

They enjoyed the evening, being playful and flirtatious. Just as they had been when they had first started dating. As the movie ended, exhaustion overtook them both. With popcorn lay strewn about, and candy littered on the floor, they both softly snored, wrapped in the warmth of their love.

When the sun rose, they both woke up to find the menu screen still playing on the TV. They attempted to stretch, but their aching backs and joints served as a reminder that they weren't teenagers anymore. Chuckling at the mess they'd made, they cleaned it up themselves and checked on their still-sleeping daughters before collapsing onto their bed.

Jason reached for his cell phone on the bedside table and noticed several missed calls from Joel, along with text messages urging him to call back. Concerned, he sat up and dialed Joel's number. Joel answered promptly.

"Sir, the Boston team has figured out the machine."

"That's great news, Joel," the president said, enthusiastic.

But Joel hesitated. "Yes, it is, but there's one problem."

"What's the problem?" he asked with a hint of concern in his voice.

Another pause. "They snuck in last night. Jesse stayed in the car while Amelia and Silas infiltrated the facility. It appears they entered through the break room door, which was propped open. From there, they gained access to the control room. They brought a hard drive and a computer, which they used to back up their data and research. They also took their notebooks, although we have already made copies of everything. Which the team is currently reviewing."

"So...what's the problem, Joel?"

"We found another notebook and a file in their system labeled 'Future Project.' The Boston team examined it and couldn't identify its connection to time travel or anything else we know of."

The president, unsure of how to proceed, inquired, "So, what does that mean? It can't be insignificant, can it?"

"We don't know yet. But when we return, the Boston team will conduct a more thorough analysis."

"They can review it, but their primary focus should remain on the machine."

Joel acknowledged and then hung up.

The Ninth Chapter: Behind Closed Doors

Silas and Amelia left the diner after breakfast, returning to his car. They sat there for a few minutes, letting the food digest. He glanced in the rearview mirror and noticed a Control officer in a nearby vehicle, waiting for them to depart.

"Amelia, go ahead and call Jesse," Silas said. "I want to hear his thoughts."

She nodded and pulled out her phone. The phone rang for a few seconds before Jesse picked up.

"Hello? Amelia?" Jesse said. "Are y'all okay?"

"Yeah, we're fine," Silas said. "Are you alone?"

"Yeah, why? What's up?"

They discussed their thoughts on how dangerous it could be if someone obtained their research and notes.

"It might be smart to see if we can go and get it," Jesse said.

"I think we need to as well," Silas said, "but I doubt they'll let us anywhere near the facility. Ever since the president and captain's visit, I feel like they're taking too much of an interest in this, especially now. We might need to do this quietly. Are you busy tonight, Jesse?"

"No. I think tonight is perfect since they think we're being good and staying at home."

"You're right, but how are we going to lose these Control guys who are constantly following us?" Amelia asked.

They all sat quietly, pondering the problem.

"I can sneak out through my backyard, walk a couple of blocks, and meet y'all," Jesse suggested. "If you can figure out a way to leave your apartment, Silas, without being spotted."

Silas considered it. "I think there's a way. Tonight, when one of them leaves to go get food, we can roll the car out while it's in neutral with the lights off since there is a slight slope by the exit."

"If you think that can work, let's go when the sun sets."

They all agreed.

With their plan in place, they spent the rest of the day about their routines, trying to maintain an air of normalcy, all while feeling the weight of their upcoming excursion.

As the sun dipped below the horizon, casting long shadows across the city, they rendezvoused at the agreed-upon location. The trio shared a nervous but determined look before embarking on their mission.

They drove cautiously, sticking to backstreets and occasionally taking alternate routes to shake off any potential pursuers. At the facility, they all exited the vehicle, and Jesse took the driver's seat to be the lookout. They each donned a single Bluetooth earphone to stay in contact via phone call. Silas carried his computer and a large external memory drive in a bag, and Amelia had an empty backpack.

They moved cautiously, staying away from street lamps and walking through the courtyard to avoid anyone. Fortunately, it was less crowded than they had anticipated. Their footsteps were silent as they approached the break room door, the same door they had used to escape the previous day. To their surprise, it was propped open. Perhaps someone had stepped out for a cigarette or to retrieve something from their car. Or maybe it was still ajar from the day before.

They peeked inside. The break room was empty. Silently, they entered, and Silas looked out, spotting a Control officer patrolling nearby. They waited until the officer entered another room before speed-walking down the hall as quickly as possible. They passed by the doors leading to the parking garage, noting the extinguished fire and the damaged cars.

Their next challenge was the entrance, guarded by Control officers to ensure no unauthorized personnel entered. They managed to sneak behind the guards unnoticed. Just as they were about to breathe a sigh of relief, someone spoke in the second room on the right. An ordinary man in jeans and a button-down shirt walked out, still on the phone, and looked away from them. However, when he turned and locked eyes with them, they were taken aback.

"Hey, are y'all here to help clean up?" the man inquired in a thick Boston accent.

Amelia and Silas exchanged bewildered glances.

"Who is it?" Jesse asked in their earphones. "What's going on?"

"Yes, we are," Silas answered.

"Well, get started down there," the Boston man said, pointing back toward the break room. "Y'all ain't supposed to be here yet. We're not done going through all the files."

"Oh yes. We're sorry," Amelia replied. "We got in earlier than we thought, and we wanted to go ahead and get started."

He eyed them briefly, waved them off, and returned to his tasks. They exhaled and resumed their journey down the hall, ultimately reaching the control room.

Silas set up his computer and external hard drive, copying files as quickly as possible, while Amelia collected vital notebooks and research papers. The urgency left no room for conversation. When he reached one file labeled "Future Project," instead of copying it, he moved it entirely, unwilling to risk anyone gaining access to it. He then informed Jesse that they were nearly finished and to prepare for their exit. Silas closed his computer and stashed it in his bag, and Amelia finished loading her backpack with documents.

As they prepared to leave, Silas had one last idea. He rushed over to the room containing The Machine, unplugged several cables, and grabbed a few items labeled "Future" and "Past Chips"—small devices used to maintain The Machine's course.

When Amelia entered the room with a quizzical expression, he simply whispered, "Let's go."

They retraced their steps from their entrance, avoiding contact with anyone they could. Jesse started the car as soon as he spotted them crossing the street. With adrenaline coursing through their veins, they sped away, driving in circles and double-checking that they weren't being followed. Eventually, they found an empty parking lot, where they parked and let out nervous laughter.

"Did you manage to grab everything?" Jesse asked, concern etched across his face.

"We got as much as we could physically, but we secured everything from the control computers," Silas replied, nodding.

His expression grew more serious. "Even *that* file?"

Silas nodded again.

"Good. We don't need anyone with that information. If it falls into the wrong hands, it could spell immense trouble for all of us."

Silas sat there, reflecting on the time he had ventured into the future. He hadn't shared a part of his experience with them at first because he was still processing it. However, he had revealed it the night before the president and captain showed up. In this future, they had made another groundbreaking discovery—not only had they improved time travel, but they had also unlocked the ability to explore various iterations of the universe. The intricate code was etched into his memory, and using a modified version of The Machine, they could access different versions of Earth.

They had kept the revelation carefully locked away, fully aware of the magnitude of its implications. But their plan to test this new code had been postponed due to the attack. And with their facility inaccessible, their plans were put on hold, especially with the uncertainty surrounding the president's involvement.

They unanimously agreed that making another copy of everything was a prudent move. They'd keep one copy at Silas's apartment, while Jesse would safeguard the other at his house. Silas copied the data from the hard drive to his computer before handing the hard drive over to Jesse.

When Silas and Amelia returned to his home, his guard slightly lowered as it seemed the security personnel had departed, presumably for a shift change. He parked his car in the lot, and they made their way back to his apartment.

After entering, Amelia suggested hiding the computer somewhere safe, to which Silas agreed. He crawled under his bed and cleverly concealed the computer between layers of bedding.

The adrenaline rush from the night's operation had left them both famished. She suggested ordering sandwiches. As she navigated a food delivery app, she inquired about alcohol, and he nodded. She added a bottle of tequila and some orange juice to the order.

While she took care of the order, Silas contacted the officer he had been in touch with earlier. The officer assured him that their team would remain stationed outside the apartment.

They both decided to shower to freshen up. Silas fetched sleepwear for both of them. A short while later, a knock came at the door, and he opened it, tipping the delivery person and collecting the food and drinks. They sat to eat in the living room, their conversation light.

"Would you like more tequila and orange juice?" Silas quipped in a goofy Boston accent, mimicking the man they had encountered earlier that day.

This prompted laughter from them, and her mouthful of food accidentally propelled across the room, making the situation even funnier. Silas ended up falling to the floor. Amelia attempted to help him up but was not strong enough, and they both tumbled down, inadvertently elbowing each other and provoking even more laughter. The alcohol may have contributed to their amusement.

After they composed themselves, they shared a tender kiss before returning to the couch. They continued to sip on their tequila and orange juice mix while watching television, deliberately avoiding any news-related content. Instead, they opted for adult cartoons filled with mindless humor.

Amelia recalled that she still hadn't finished cleaning the sheets from that morning and, in her slightly inebriated state, got up. "Where are your extra sheets?"

"In the closet next to the front door," he replied.

As she walked toward the closet, a magnet on the fridge

caught her attention—an unfamiliar magnet that she hadn't noticed during her previous visits. It resembled one that one might obtain at a convention or from an insurance company, displaying a calendar.

When she went back to Silas and asked about it, he, who had never realized it was there, appeared perplexed.

"I don't know. I never put that there," he replied.

He rose, but she shot him a sharp glance that made him stay put. She turned back to him and signaled him to watch TV while mouthing, "Act normal."

She couldn't shake the feeling that something was off, that the magnet was thicker than usual. She walked back over to inspect it. It was indeed thicker than the average calendar magnet. When she looked from the side, she saw a piece of tinted glass within the O.

She carefully backed away toward the closet, contemplating her next move. After opening the closet, she retrieved some sheets. "Hey, Silas. Do you mind helping me make the bed?"

His eyes widened as he caught on. "Of course, Amelia."

They both walked into his bedroom.

Once inside, she whispered, "Are you certain you've never seen that magnet before? Like a hundred percent sure?"

He stood there, now sobered, contemplating it. "No. I've never seen that there. Why?"

"Okay. That's not good. There appears to be a camera lens inside the O."

"A camera? From where or who? Why?"

It dawned on them simultaneously.

"The president," they whispered in unison.

The weight of this revelation hung in the room as they processed its implications. The idea that the president might have them under surveillance in Silas's home filled them with unease. Silas's mind raced, pondering whether it was just a camera or if it could also record audio. He couldn't help but wonder about the presence of other cameras.

Amelia grabbed the magnet from the fridge and examined it for any clues.

He urged her to put it back, emphasizing the importance of not alerting the president of their discovery. "We can't let him know that we know it's here," he mouthed.

She agreed and returned the magnet to its original spot.

"If he is monitoring us, it means he's up to something. What if there are others?" she asked, prompting them to conduct a thorough search of the apartment.

They primarily focused on the bedroom but found nothing that appeared suspicious.

"I don't see anything. It's possible this magnet was just recently placed here," she said.

Silas couldn't shake the feeling of being violated.

They both agreed to continue their night as if it was normal but to let Jesse know so he could check his house. Silas cleaned up their trash, while she went to make the bed. But before doing so, she texted Jesse everything that had happened. After she sent the text, Silas walked in.

"What if they are reading our texts and listening to our phone calls?" she asked.

He sat on the unmade bed and thought about it. "Well, I'm sure they've been doing that for a long time already, so I'm not going to worry about that too much right now. Right now, we need to make sure we are safe and acting as normal as possible."

Her phone buzzed. It was Jesse. He let them know that he would check his house and would update them, but he didn't think so because his wife had been home the last few days.

Silas got up and helped Amelia make the bed. They then closed the door, and he handed her a glass. On the bed, they sat, filled with a whirlwind of thoughts about what the hell was going on.

"Do you think he's after The Machine?" Silas asked.

Amelia took a sip of her drink. "I think so, which makes this even more difficult. If we are going to get ahead of him, we have to pretend like we don't know anything."

He nodded. "You're right," he said with a sigh. "We've been cautious so far, and that's kept us safe. But now we need to be even more careful."

She leaned against him, seeking comfort in his presence. "I just can't believe this is happening," she murmured. "I never thought we'd be caught up in something like this."

He put his arm around her, pulling her closer. "None of us did," he said softly. "But we'll figure this out. We have each other's backs. We'll find a way to outmaneuver the president."

They lay next to each other, overwhelmed by the uncertainty of what the future might hold. Her phone buzzed. It was Jesse confirming that there were no cameras or recording devices at his house. She replied with a thumbs-up and tossed her phone to the end of the bed with a sigh.

"Do you think they bugged my house?" she asked. "I mean, it doesn't really matter since we're never over there…"

"No, I don't think they did. I think he has more of an interest in me. I don't know why, but I think he does."

They lay next to each other, the television softly playing in the background, until exhaustion overcame them, and they drifted off to sleep.

The Tenth Chapter: Stakes in Secrets

Sitting in front of the computer, Captain Joel lurked, monitoring the facility's camera feeds with a few of his officers. He had started watching as soon as he had received word that the three had broken into the facility. They informed him that one person was in the car while the other two were inside the building. He instructed the team to not interfere, wanting to see if they would take any action regarding the Future Project file.

Nothing particularly interesting happened though. They eventually left, and a while later, he received a call about Silas and Amelia being home and having ordered food, which didn't appear out of the ordinary.

"Captain!" one of the officers said. "We might have an issue. They found the camera in the apartment."

The captain switched cameras and watched the situation unfold as Silas and Amelia attempted to discreetly deal with the camera's discovery. For geniuses, they weren't very clever. He chuckled to himself.

"What should we do, sir?" an officer asked.

He contemplated his options. "Let's give them a scare," he said. "Get Torres dressed in civilian clothes and instruct him to break into the apartment tonight and create a convincing impression of a robbery—nothing physical, just enough to make them believe it. He should take Silas's wallet and any other belongings he can find, and perhaps break something to wake them up. Once he notices they're awake, tell him to leave."

The officer relayed the instructions to Officer Torres and then contacted the team outside Silas's apartment to let them know he was coming.

At three a.m., Torres arrived at the apartment and got the go-ahead from the captain.

Silas and Amelia were sound asleep, completely unaware of what was happening on the other side of the bedroom door. A loud crash shattered their silence, jolting them awake. They exchanged worried glances in the dark. He quickly scanned the room, remembered there was a bat under his bed, and retrieved it. He then stealthily approached the bedroom door.

Slowly, he opened the door and saw a large intruder, who hadn't noticed him yet, standing in the hallway. He widened the door just enough to fit through, raised the bat, and swung it at the intruder's head. The bat connected, causing the intruder to stumble and yell out.

"FUCK! What the hell, man?!"

The intruder turned around, and Silas got a better look at his face. Silas attempted to swing the bat again, but he caught it and effortlessly wrestled it out of Silas's grasp.

Silas, not sure what else to do, shouted, "Get out! Get out of my apartment!"

The intruder, bleeding from his head, hesitated. He then tossed the bat aside, and it shattered the living room window, creating a spiderweb-like pattern. "Watch yourself," he warned before leaving.

Silas and Amelia were left bewildered. She called the officer in charge to report the incident. Within a few minutes, two officers from Control arrived at their door. They recounted the events to the officers, who took photos and filed a report.

The officers mentioned that this had become a crime scene, which puzzled Silas and Amelia since it appeared to be a simple robbery. They advised them to stay elsewhere for their safety. She suggested going to her place, and he agreed. He hurried to his room, packed a bag with clothes, and discreetly stashed the computer inside it. The officers then informed them that extra personnel would be sent to their current location and to Amelia's house per the captain's orders.

Amelia and Silas exchanged glances again, now grappling with a mix of fear and uncertainty. They couldn't help but wonder about the intruder's intentions and what had prompted this intrusion.

As they prepared to leave the apartment under Control's watchful eyes, Amelia couldn't help but feel a creeping sense of vulnerability. "Silas," she whispered, "do you think this is related to what we found on the fridge?"

He paused for a moment, contemplating the possibility. "It's hard to say," he replied in a hushed tone. "But one thing's for sure: we're dealing with something far bigger and more dangerous than we ever imagined."

A lingering sense of unease accompanied their departure. They knew they needed to tread carefully and watch their every step as they navigated this treacherous terrain.

Amelia and Silas got into his car. Security followed them all the way to her house. Her driveway was already accompanied by several unmarked vehicles, which they assumed belonged to Control. Inside, she turned on the lights, and he went to her bedroom and set his bag on her bed.

The first thing they did before saying anything was scan the apartment for anything that looked like a camera or a recording device. After a few hours of searching, they found nothing. They could breathe again. They locked all the doors, and she closed the curtains and placed a chair in front of the front door.

She then joined Silas in her bedroom, where he had taken his computer out of the bag. They both agreed to send a message to Jesse to let him know what had happened, even though he probably wouldn't be awake at this hour.

After she sent him the long message, Silas said, "I think we need some sleep after tonight."

She nodded. They didn't know how they could be so tired after the ordeal they had just gone through. They both crawled into bed.

She looked at him and gasped. "Silas, you have blood on your face and in your hair!"

He got up and went to the bathroom mirror. It wasn't a lot of blood. Just speckled.

"Go shower, so you can get that washed off."

He stripped his clothes and noticed some on his shirt as well. He got in the shower, and she grabbed some clothes out of his bag. She joined him, thinking she could clean off what had happened that night.

They both enjoyed the warm water and then got dressed. She was glad she could wear her own clothes again. Finally, they got into bed and fell asleep.

A knock at the door woke them. Amelia glanced over at her clock, which read 8:38 a.m. They were both still exhausted from the night before.

"I'll go check the door and see if Jesse responded," Silas said.

He got out of bed, moved the chair from the front door, and opened it.

A Control officer. "The investigation is nearly over. They are cleaning everything up today, and you all should be able to return to the facility tomorrow. Have a good day." He then turned around and left.

Silas closed the door and returned to the bedroom to inform Amelia.

She sighed. "*Finally*. Oh, Jesse responded. He asked if we were okay, and I let him know that we are at my house. He mentioned that there weren't any disturbances, but a guard did show up this morning to tell him what you just told me, along with the news that our apartment was robbed."

He nodded.

"So, what do we do today?"

"I don't know what else we can do." He sat on the bed and grabbed his laptop, which he turned on. He stared at it for a while.

She looked at him curiously, wondering what he was doing.

He clicked on the file labeled "Future Project." He sat there, reading over the data, the codes, and the notes. However, he still couldn't figure out how they could implement this into The Machine they already had. "This will have to be done as a group at a later time," he said, sounding frustrated as he shut his computer and put it back in his backpack.

"I don't know why we would be using this in the future," he continued. "I'm still confused as to why I was given this. I'm sure it has some great importance, but we can't do anything about it until we get back into the facility. And hopefully, nothing is beyond repair there." He sighed.

"This sucks, and it's all very fishy," she said. "I think we need to collect our thoughts and get with Jesse. Maybe we can go over there and try to figure out what the president's plan is."

Silas nodded. "You're right. We need to piece together what's going on. But we have to act like we don't know."

She got up from the bed and stretched, feeling the tension from the past few days dissipate. "First, let's call Jesse since he's awake and see about going over to his house. Maybe he can think of something. If not, it'll be better if we are all together, putting our brains together."

Silas called Jesse while she changed. As the phone rang, he stared at her, engrossed in her beauty. He was so lost in the moment that he didn't hear Jesse answer the phone at first. When she finished getting dressed, Silas hung up the phone.

"Jesse said to come over a bit later," he said. "He will see if he can find anything about the president online. He also said to let him know when we're on our way."

Amelia nodded. "Great. I'm going to finish getting ready while you change. I'll go make something for us to eat too."

Silas pulled out some jeans and a shirt from his bag while she put some makeup on in the bathroom. She didn't wear a lot; Silas barely noticed any at all. In the kitchen, he sat as she made some breakfast. Nothing fancy, just toast, eggs, and some fruit. It was a nice change of pace from the takeout they had the last few days. They sat and ate, enjoying each other's company.

Silas's mind wandered back to the robber and what he had said. It was such an odd thing to say. He brought this up to Amelia, and she agreed it was quite odd.

"What could he mean by that?" she asked. "Was it a threat or what?"

He shrugged. "It was probably nothing. He might have been

on something. But he was really built if he was on drugs."

They finished their breakfast. He got up and washed their dishes while she dried and put them away. He glanced at the clock. 9:51 a.m. Still a few hours before they would head over to Jesse.

"Want to go get some coffee?" he asked. "I need to get gas before we go to Jesse's anyway."

She nodded. "I could use some coffee."

They returned to her room, where they both collected a few things. Afterward, they left, letting the guard outside know their plans. He called someone to follow them around, but she questioned the necessity of it—without receiving a response.

"Not the brightest group, huh?" she remarked once they got in Silas's car.

They both shared a laugh. He backed out of the driveway and drove down the road, heading to the gas station first. He filled up his car while she went inside to pick up a few items.

As he was filling up, someone two pumps away caught his eye. It was the *same guy* who had robbed them last night. He froze—not because the man was there but because he wore a Control shirt. He stood there, staring, while the man remained unaware of his presence. Eventually, he snapped a few pictures of the man with his phone.

He sent the photos to Jesse and Amelia. "THAT'S HIM! THAT'S THE GUY WHO BROKE IN LAST NIGHT!!!"

He looked toward the gas station store and saw Amelia at the counter, her face filled with shock. He glanced back at the pump two pumps away, but the man was no longer there. He then spotted the man heading toward the store.

Amelia saw him approaching as well and wondered if he recognized her. Of course, he must, right? She asked the attendant if she could use the bathroom, left her items on the counter, and hurried there.

Silas replaced the gas nozzle, got in his car, and started it. His phone rang. A call from Amelia.

"I'm in the bathroom," she said. "Is he still in the store?"

"Yes." He looked over. "Wait. He's walking to the back. Stay there."

They stayed silent as he kept an eye on the man's movements. He updated her when the man paid for his purchase at the counter. Afterward, he ducked to avoid being seen as the man returned to his vehicle and got inside. With a sigh, he informed Amelia that it was safe to come out.

She paid for her items and ran to his car. "What was that?!?!"

"I don't know!" he responded, equally puzzled.

"So, it was about the camera? Maybe? Was this a scare tactic then?"

"I don't know…" He glanced at the pictures he had taken, attempting to make sense of the situation. "It's too much of a coincidence," he muttered. "'Watch yourself…'" He turned to her. "I don't think this is a coincidence. I believe it was all a threat to keep us in line, to maintain our friendship with the president. I also suspect that the attack wasn't entirely the work of the cult."

She sat there, trying to process everything. "We need to discuss all of this with Jesse. We need his help."

The atmosphere inside the car was tense as they got their coffee and contemplated the bizarre events from the past few days.

At Jesse's house, guards greeted them and allowed them to park on the street. Jesse warmly embraced them both and welcomed them inside. They received hugs from Jesse's wife and daughter and were offered something to drink.

Jesse led them into his office, and Silas placed his bag next to a chair. A few minutes later, Jesse's wife, Sandra, entered with Amelia's tea and a glass of water for Silas.

"If you don't mind giving us a few minutes, we need to talk about work," Jesse said.

Sandra nodded. Silas assumed that Jesse had informed her about most, if not all, of what had transpired in the last few days. She left the room and closed the door behind her. He and Amelia proceeded to fill Jesse in on everything, including the details that couldn't be conveyed through text messages.

Jesse took a sip of his drink. "This won't do."

Silas and Amelia exchanged puzzled glances.

He rose from his seat, reached into a cabinet, and retrieved a bottle of whiskey along with three elegant glasses. He poured a glass for each of them.

He took a strong sip, and Silas and Amelia followed suit.

"What's our plan?" he asked, his tone filled with determination.

The Eleventh Chapter: Speed Bump

Sitting at his desk, President Jason King had nothing else planned for the day since Captain Joel and the Boston team weren't coming in until later that day. He opened his laptop and pulled up the camera footage, wondering what the trio had taken. He had already reviewed the facility's camera footage, but he couldn't see everything they took.

He then wondered if they brought whatever they had taken to Silas's apartment. Opening the footage, he clicked on the date and scrolled through the time, watching them quickly move around the apartment and then leave. A few hours later, they returned with two very heavy bags.

He continued watching the footage—as they talked, ate, or acted uncomfortably cute, which annoyed him. Amelia got up from the couch and disappeared, but Silas, in his drunken state, had a peculiar expression on his face and looked right at the magnet. A few minutes later, the camera moved and pointed at Amelia's face as if she was searching for something. She then put it back on the fridge.

The president was certainly caught, but he wondered why they would put the magnet back. Unless they didn't want him to know…

He continued watching as they returned to the bedroom

and closed the door. He fast-forwarded the footage to find a peculiar sight—someone breaking in. That person picked up a glass and threw it on the floor. Odd.

Out of nowhere, Silas swung a bat right at the intruder's head. The man appeared to yell, bleeding. The president recognized this man; he had seen him with Captain Joel before. The man mouthed something to Silas and then left.

But why would a man who worked for Joel be there? If the trio recognized him, they would start piecing everything together.

The president closed his laptop. "I'm going to bring this up to Joel."

Since it was about lunchtime, he decided to have lunch with his family. As they enjoyed their pizza together, Jason received a text, indicating that Joel and the Boston team were flying back to DC. He promptly replied to Joel, expressing his desire for a briefing upon their return. Joel responded with a thumbs-up emoji and mentioned that he would inform Jason when they landed.

They finished their pizza, and he instructed the girls to go finish their schoolwork. They attempted to argue, but a stern look from their mom made them comply.

"I'm going to have another meeting with Joel later," Jason said. "After the recent attack, he wants to provide me with a briefing. I also need to prepare a speech regarding these attacks for the press and the public. I want to convey that we are doing everything in our power."

"Do you think you'll be home for dinner at least?" Sarah asked. "I know you're a busy man, but I've enjoyed the quiet the last day or two. I was starting to get used to it."

Jason smiled. "I miss the old days. Money was tighter, but

things were easier. I wouldn't trade what we have today with the position we're in, but there are days when I miss the quiet."

"Some days, I do too." She smiled in return. "But I love you so much for everything you've done for us." She leaned in and kissed him.

"You are my rock, love," he whispered, holding her close.

Their moment of affection served as a poignant reminder of the unbreakable bond. Yet as they sat there, savoring the comfort of each other's presence, Jason's secretary walked in.

"I'm so sorry to bother you two," she said with a friendly smile, "but the media team would like to go over the speech for later."

"It's okay," Sarah said. "Go ahead."

He gave her a quick kiss and then followed his secretary to his office, where the team was already waiting on the couches. Over the next hour, they meticulously went through the speech to fine-tune every word, making it more appealing to the public and to sound more natural for him.

After several rounds of revisions and discussions, he received a text from Joel, notifying him that they had landed. He apologized, cutting the speech meeting short, and expressed his gratitude.

Jason then called the kitchen and requested a few bottles of his favorite cola, along with some ice. He also retrieved a bottle of whiskey and glasses from his desk drawer. A young woman entered the room, carrying the bottles and a small bucket of ice. He gestured for her to place them on the coffee table.

On his television screen, he displayed an image of the man who had broken into Silas's apartment. Just as he received word from the gate that Joel had arrived, he took a seat on the couch, facing the door, and waited.

Joel entered the room about fifteen minutes later, his gaze drawn to the screen. He sighed, sat on the opposite side of the couch, poured himself a glass of whiskey, and took a sip.

"I did what needed to be done," he said. "They found the magnet. I wanted them to focus more on the break-in and forget about the camera."

"Yeah, and how well did that work?" Jason responded. "Did he think to take the magnet while the fake robbery happened?"

"From the looks of it, it scared them pretty good."

Jason grew agitated. "Well, if they didn't suspect us when they found the magnet, they definitely do now! How foolish can you be?"

"How dare you, sir?! I followed your orders!"

"You're right. You did. *And then* you took matters into your own hands," the president snapped. "They were drunk! We could've just left it alone. We could've waited until they left the house and replaced it with the same magnet but with no camera! Also, don't you dare question me!"

Both men sat there for a few minutes, simmering with anger.

"You're right," Joel said. "I took it into my own hands, but I did what I thought was right. I did what needed to be done!"

"You need to get rid of him. Hide him. Move him somewhere else. Because if they run into him or recognize him, we are done being their friends. We go from gaining helpful people to doing this on our own, which will make life so much more difficult for us!"

"You know what, sir?" Joel took a sip. "I do need to get rid of him." He made a call, and the man from the screen, Torres, walked into the room. "Torres, this is the president. He would love to have a word with you. Please have a seat."

Torres closed the door behind him and sat next to Captain

Joel.

"Here, Torres. Have a drink. The president isn't too happy with us. We need to convince him that we do what is best at all times."

He remained silent, taking the offered drink.

"Now, how can we convince him that this won't happen again, Torres?"

He still gave no spoken response. Instead, he placed the glass down and looked at the president, who showed no emotion. In an instant, he pulled out his knife and cut his own throat. He bled out, keeping eye contact with the president the whole time, before collapsing forward onto the edge of the coffee table. He slid off and slumped to the floor.

A faint gurgling escaped his lips.

"So, problem solved. Any other requests, Jason?" Joel inquired.

Jason, still reeling from the turn of events, stared at the lifeless body on the floor. An eerie silence filled the room, only broken by the clinking of glass. He looked up and saw Joel pouring them each a glass of whiskey.

"Drink," Joel said.

He accepted the drink, his hand slightly shaking, and slammed it back. The gruesome act was etched into his mind. He knew the world was ruthless, but he never would have thought he would witness something like this. Taking another deep breath, he asked, "Why would he do that to himself?"

Joel leaned back, the weight of their situation apparent in his expression. "Well, that's the thing, Jason. You might be the president, and you might think you have all the power in the world, but I lead a secretive group. Not only do I lead but I have complete control. What I say is the word. If I tell them to jump, they will do it without question. If I instruct them to carry out unspeakable acts, they do it until it's done or until they're dead. If I order them to end their own lives because they've messed up, they don't question it. The people, the civilians of this country, question everything you say, Mr. President. They question anything you ask of them. But my people? There is no question. At the end of the day, it's just done. This is what power is, Jason. This is control."

Joel's words hung in the room, a stark reminder of the darkness that lurked beneath the surface of their world.

Jason just sat there in shock.

A few minutes later, four men entered the room with a body bag, cleaning supplies, and carpet. Within twenty minutes, they had placed Torres's body in a body bag, replaced the section of carpet he had bled on, and wiped away the blood that had made its way onto the couch and table.

As if nothing had happened.

Joel thanked them, and they left just as smoothly as they had arrived. Jason opened his mouth to speak, but he interrupted.

"Come on, Jason. As long as you've known me, I would never hurt you or your family. I need you as much as you need me. I handle cleaning up the messes and resolving your problems, and in return, you help keep my team funded and under the radar. Why would I want to ruin a partnership like that?"

His words carried a sense of assurance, reminding Jason of the complex web that bound them together.

Jason sighed, contemplating the dangerous nature of his partnership. Perhaps this was the way it was meant to be—he as the public face and Joel handling the covert operations.

"You're right, Joel," he admitted. "But here's the thing: we need to exercise extreme caution moving forward. We can't afford another slipup or any more risks."

Joel nodded. "Agreed. There won't be any more mistakes moving forward. My team understands the consequences of failure, and we won't allow another incident like Torres."

They finished their drinks, and Joel provided an update on their findings. He mentioned that there would be more information once the Boston research team had settled into the nearby lab.

"Tell them to go ahead and attempt to build the machine," Jason instructed. "We'll consider it a backup plan."

Joel nodded. Furthermore, he informed Jason that the trio would return to their facility tomorrow. He had ensured that the place was cleaned up, leaving no trace of the recent events.

With everything in order, Jason yawned, just realizing how tired he was. He stood, indicating that the meeting was over, and they both shook hands.

"Joel, I appreciate your swift action," he said, "but if you ever have someone take their life in my presence again, I will drop the program and end everything you know so fast that you won't know what hit you."

Joel stood there, not intimidated by the threat. Instead, he decided to play along. "You're right, sir. That won't happen again." He winked. "I'll call you tomorrow with any updates, Mr. President."

He then left, leaving Jason feeling cold and overwhelmed. His body finally seemed to catch up with what had happened. He rushed to his trashcan and vomited, expelling pizza, cola, and whiskey.

After wiping his mouth with a napkin, Jason realized he needed to rest. He had a press conference in the morning. As he left, the cleaning crew came in, and he apologized for the mess. They dismissed it and wished him a good night.

He returned to his bedroom, where his wife was reading. After a shower, he joined Sarah on the bed.

"Are you okay, honey?" she asked.

"Yeah, I'm fine. Just not feeling good."

She looked at him with concern but decided not to pry.

The girls ran in and jumped on him.

He hugged and kissed them. "Time for bed, girls."

They both groaned, complaining that it's still early.

Sarah and Jason laughed.

"No, it's a school night," she said. "Off to bed. We will come tuck you in in a minute. That room better be clean."

They scurried off to clean up their toys.

Sarah continued to read for a few more minutes, and he watched her, both familiar with this routine. They later tucked the girls in and said goodnight. Returning to their room, they both got into bed.

"I don't know what's bothering you, but you seem off," she said. "If you don't want to talk about it now, that's fine, but you'll need to talk about it eventually. Don't hide things from me. I love you."

He sat there for a moment. "I'll tell you eventually, but right now, I just want to be here with you." He smiled and kissed her.

She understood, kissing him in return.

He held her as she continued to read. Eventually, he drifted off to sleep.

The next morning was like any other. He and his wife woke up, got ready for the day, and prepared their daughters for the day ahead. After breakfast, he headed to his office to prepare for the press conference. He briefly went over his lines with his media team, ensuring he was well-prepared. Although teleprompters would be available, they wanted his delivery to sound natural and unscripted.

About an hour later, his secretary entered and informed him that it was time to proceed to the press room. They all got up and followed him down the hall, passing various doors. He greeted those he passed with a friendly hello and good morning. Just outside the door where he would enter, they stopped.

Jason took a deep breath and assumed his "presidential" demeanor, ready to face the cameras and the questions. As he opened the door, a barrage of camera flashes and questions met him.

He walked up the stage, taking his place behind the podium. "Good morning, everyone," he began, and the room fell silent. "I hope you're all having a great day today. I'm pleased to see each and every one of you." He smiled, though there was little response.

As the room remained quiet, he continued. "Well, let's get started then." He began his speech.

He expressed concern about the terrorist cult and the need to end the attacks. Assuring everyone that his top team was working on it. In truth, it all felt like a charade to him as he had more important matters at hand. He was willing to do whatever it took to achieve his goals, but for the public, he had to project a caring and responsible image.

Throughout the speech, he maintained his composed demeanor, speaking with conviction and clarity. He emphasized the resilience of the American people, their ability to overcome adversity, and their unwavering determination to protect their way of life. He praised the law enforcement and the intelligence community, highlighting their relentless efforts to bring those responsible for the attacks to justice.

To conclude his speech, he called for a moment of silence to honor the victims of the recent attacks. The room fell silent as everyone bowed their heads in solemn reflection.

He then took questions from reporters, answering with poise and confidence. He remained steadfast in his commitment to transparency and pledged to keep the public informed of any developments.

Walking back to his office, he couldn't help but acknowledge the necessity of falsehoods. It wasn't the first time he had to wear a mask for the public, and he understood the susceptibility the masses were to manipulation.

Joel called. "Hey, I think the Boston team has made a breakthrough," he said. "You should come by. It's not built yet, but they believe it's feasible."

"Good news," Jason responded. "Let them know they'll have all the funds they require to get it done. Start building."

After ending the call, he informed his secretary of his imminent meeting with Control to discuss updates on an ongoing investigation. She nodded and arranged for the security team to prepare the vehicles. He also sent a text to his wife, notifying her that he would be back soon.

Jason got into an unmarked vehicle, and they set off for the laboratory, which was cleverly disguised as an old bread factory that had been abandoned for the last five years.

The ride was relatively quiet with bustling vehicles on the highway and winding roads, but his mind raced. If the Boston team had indeed made significant strides, it meant one step closer to achieving his goal. The machine would render the trio obsolete. The power he would wield would transcend mere politics, surpassing the mundane meetings filled with bickering and complaints. This device would grant him ultimate authority, and with it, he could shape the world.

The entrance appeared like any other gate. However, it was guarded by Control, and Jason's heart quickened. He knew that within those walls lay the culmination of his ambitions—a power that could reshape his world.

The guards waved them through, and the vehicle entered a rough-looking building that had an old bread company name fading on its side. Jason disembarked, while his driver remained in the vehicle.

The old factory had been transformed into a hive of activity. Scientists and engineers bustled about, their faces illuminated by the soft glow of computer screens.

Joel met Jason near the entrance and led him through a labyrinth of corridors and to an empty office, which appeared to have once been the factory manager's office. Jason questioned the presence of so many people as he had believed there were only five involved in the project.

As he posed the question, a tall man entered the room. "Hello, sir. My name is William, but you can call me Will. To answer your question, yes, some of us are from the Boston facility. However, we had to bring in additional personnel because upon reviewing our initial attempts and understanding this project's complexity, we realized we need experts from various parts of Europe and Russia. It was necessary to ensure the project's success, and, like Torres, they have all signed non-disclosure agreements."

Joel chimed in with a chuckle. "Yes, we needed more staff, and it doesn't hurt to have extra security through NDAs."

"Good," Jason said. "Please update me on the time line and the necessary tasks."

William handed him a small packet that detailed everything that needed to be done, accompanied by a schedule with estimated timeframes. "Well, Mr. President, based on the information we have and your available resources, we believe we can have it completed within a week and ready for testing."

His eyes widened. "In just a week? That quickly?"

"That's correct. That's our estimated date if everything goes smoothly. We've arranged for all team members to stay in a nearby hotel to minimize travel time, and Control will keep a close eye on them. We've listed all the necessary items we require, and if we manage to order everything by the end of today, we should have it within two to three days. Then we can build and implement the code as soon as the components arrive."

He nodded, impressed by the team's efficiency and dedication. "Excellent. It seems like we're making good progress. I appreciate your hard work. Please keep me updated on any developments."

"We will make sure everything proceeds smoothly, Mr. President," Joel added. He waved a pocketknife in a taunting manner, reminding Jason of the incident the night prior.

Jason got up, and Joel walked him out of the room.

The area now seemed much clearer now. He could visualize it: the machine over there with computers and wires hooked up to it. A team standing nearby, ready to assist him in traveling into the future to gain insights and manipulate it for his own benefit. Or to assist him in journeying into the past to amass wealth and popularity.

As he left the laboratory, the weight of the world seemed

to press down on his shoulders. However, that heavy burden was soon forgotten by the fact that the power he sought was now within his grasp—just a week away. With each passing moment, he moved closer to his goal.

On his way back, he instructed his driver to stop at a small flower shop. Secret Service agents ensured it was safe before he entered. Once given the all clear, he carefully selected bouquets of flowers for his wife and daughters. The shop's owner insisted on giving them away for free, but he politely declined. He did, however, agree to take a photo with the owner and employees, knowing it would bring positive publicity to the store. After expressing his gratitude, he left and headed home.

As the vehicles sped down the highway, a nagging feeling of moral crept back into his subconscious. He recognized that people would suffer because of his choices. Success and power often came at a cost. But he pushed those thoughts aside, unwilling to dwell on the consequences.

Upon arriving home, he found his wife and daughters working on their schoolwork, particularly math. A subject he had never favored. When they turned and saw him holding the beautiful bouquets, their faces lit up with delight.

His wife greeted him with a kiss, grateful for the surprise. "Thank you so much for these flowers, honey. They're so lovely." She laughed. "I feel like I'm a teenager again, receiving those daisies from my mom's garden. My mother wasn't too happy because it took her forever to grow them, but I didn't care. They were beautiful." Although a hint of worry crossed her mind. "Why the surprise? Did something happen?"

With a reassuring smile, he kissed her back and then planted a kiss on his daughters' heads. "No. Nothing bad happened. The future is just going to be amazing."

The Twelfth Chapter: Yesterday Is Tomorrow's Mistakes

Amelia's alarm went off at eight a.m. She turned over and hit the side of Silas's head with her pillow. "Turn that damn thing off," she said with an exhausted voice.

He woke up with a start. "We've got to get up and go back to work, Amelia…"

They slowly got up.

They had spent all afternoon and most of the night at Jesse's house. From what they had gathered, they couldn't trust the president nor anyone working for him. They knew that ignoring the president's help from here on out would be dangerous, but they'd just have to figure that out. Their plan was to continue their work because their goal was still to help the people. Jesse had let them know that he had started coming up with a plan, but he wasn't ready to let them in on it just yet.

Amelia and Silas shared worried looks as they prepared for the day ahead. The weight of their decision to distance themselves from the president and Control hung on their minds. They couldn't help but wonder if they were making the right choice.

While eating breakfast, Amelia spoke up, her voice full of concern. "Silas, do you ever think we're making a mistake?

What if we're underestimating the president's influence?"

He sighed. "I've had the same thoughts. But we can't forget why we started this work in the first place. We must stay true to our principles and what we believe is right."

She nodded. "You're right. We can't let fear dictate our choices. Let's focus on our research and trust that Jesse will come up with a plan that keeps us safe."

With renewed resolve, they finished breakfast and headed to work, ready to face the uncertain future that lay ahead.

As they pulled up to the facility, it appeared as though it had never been attacked. The only sign left was some burnt concrete in the parking garage. Whatever Control did, it looked immaculate.

Jesse's vehicle was already there. Silas and Amelia grabbed their belongings and entered the facility, which was bustling with most of their team. Some Control officers still walked about, giving them an uneasy feeling. They made their way to the control room for The Machine, where they found Jesse flipping through papers.

"Hey, bud," Silas said. "What's going on?"

"Huh?" Jesse looked up. "Oh, hey, guys. I'm just going over a few things."

They set their bags down, and Silas took the parts he had stolen from The Machine the other day back.

The trio continued working on improving The Machine while also examining what had been taken by Control. A few hours later, they discovered that nearly everything they had been working on over the past few years had been copied and stolen.

Jesse stood and paced. "What could he be using this for? Is there anything happening in the world? Impending war? Financial crisis? A move toward one government? Knowledge?"

"What are you talking about, Jesse?" Amelia asked.

He ignored her, concern etched on his face.

"Power," Silas said.

He looked at him with wide eyes.

"Power. Think about it. On the outside, he seems like a family-oriented man, caring for his people. But think. The power move he made at the restaurant, knowing when and where we would be—power. The theory that he's attacking us with actors dressed as cult members and offering us protection to gain our trust—power. Making sure we have that non-stop protection but also keeping eyes and ears on us—power. The false robbery because we found a camera—power. It's always been about power."

Jesse turned to him with a smile. "Now you understand why I don't trust the government."

"No, that can't be," Amelia said. "I mean, I don't trust the president as far as I can throw him, but for him to kill his own guards to win us over and control us…"

They both looked at her.

"This isn't the first time, Amelia," Jesse said. "The government has done that many times. It's all about doing whatever they can. They'll take the sacrifice and falsify some sad story. And the media has been in their pocket since the turn of the century. Who's going to go against the president?"

As the weight of their discoveries settled in, a palpable tension filled the room. The trio realized they were not just up against a corrupt leader but a government machinery fueled by unchecked power and deception.

Silas, his voice tinged with frustration, continued, "We need to expose this. We can't let them control us any longer."

Amelia nodded, determination flashing in her eyes. "So, what's our next move? How do we take on the most powerful man in the country?"

"I have a theory," Jesse said. "Think about Silas's first time travel. As a turkey, he had this massive battle with humans that could have made a huge change in history. But it didn't. In history books, it was just a bunch of birds attacking humans, and no one was injured. It only lasted a few minutes until someone fired a rifle, and they fluttered away. What I believe is that no matter what happens, we cannot make major changes. Time is meant to follow a singular time line. It will not allow us to drastically alter the future."

The room fell silent as his theory sank in. It was a sobering thought—the idea that they might be bound by some unseen force. The responsibility they carried seemed even greater now.

Silas leaned forward, his expression contemplative. "So, you're saying that no matter what we do, we can't alter the course of history?"

Jesse nodded. "That's what I believe. It's like there are safeguards in place to ensure the time line remains intact. We can make small changes, but nothing that would cause a ripple effect."

"But if we can't change history," Amelia said, "how do we stop the president from using our research for his gain?"

"Maybe it's not about changing history but exposing the truth," Silas said. "If we can't prevent him from taking our research, we can at least make sure the world knows what he's doing with it."

With a renewed sense of purpose, the trio formulated a plan. Their mission was clear: they might not be able to alter history, but they could certainly influence its course.

As they worked, Amelia spoke. "So what does it matter if he can use The Machine? If he cannot alter what happens besides small things, that would not change the time line."

Jesse sat up. "Here is the thing: it's not the past I'm too worried about. It's the future. He can go into the future, see what's to come, and then try to alter the present. Since that hasn't happened yet, things can change. The versions of ourselves in the future, for instance, can't come back to today and change what will happen to them in their present time line. Time can only go forward."

Amelia pondered his explanation for a moment. "So, you're saying that while the past is relatively safe from major changes, the future remains vulnerable?"

He nodded, his expression grave. "Exactly. And given the president's hunger for power, he might attempt to reshape the future to his advantage, even if it means drastic consequences for others."

"Then our mission is even more critical," Silas said. "We need to figure out a way to stop him one way or another."

"How do we stop him if exposure doesn't work or if that does not become an option for us?" she asked. "Like what? Do we need to just show up at the White House and tell him no?"

"I don't know yet," Jesse admitted. "I do know that showing up at where he runs the country will not go well."

"Well, he has to have a facility of some sort to do this in, right?" Silas asked.

"Do you think we can just walk in and say, 'Hey, everyone. Don't do that?' We are only three people up against many, many more."

They all sat there, contemplating the enormous challenge

ahead.

"What if…" Silas paused. "What if we can figure out how to go back in time and delve into someone's body who was here, someone who is part Control when they were copying all our information to take back to the president? Then we can figure out where the lab is. What do you both think?"

Amelia nodded, thinking it could be possible.

"We got close last time," Jesse said, "but we will need to put the next few days into this, writing the code to mark the right person and subdue them with your subconscious at the right time."

"What about the Boston man?" Amelia asked.

"Yeah. Him." Silas nodded. "He was here the night we broke in. We know what time he was in the room. I don't remember his name though. I don't remember seeing a badge or anything."

"We can get the camera footage, and if we manage to get a picture of him, we can perform a reverse search on the internet to find his social media profiles and his name."

"Even if we do obtain all of that, we still need to write the code to ensure its accuracy," Jesse said.

"I know, Jesse, but it's a starting point."

"Okay. *That's* the starting point. Amelia, go get the footage and find our Bostonian man. Silas, you and I will work on the code. Maybe we can make significant progress before she's finished. Once you're done, Amelia, we'll need your help."

Both she and Silas nodded in agreement.

The Thirteenth Chapter: Unlucky

"We did it," Amelia muttered as her latest test came back positive.

The trio were hunched over their computers with heavy bags under their eyes. Empty cans of energy drinks and disposable coffee cups littered the area. All from four days of relentless work.

"What?!" Jesse and Silas asked in unison.

"This is it! We did it!" She stood, holding the laptop. Her back and knees popped as she straightened after hours of immobility.

"Let me see," Silas said. He took the computer, scanned it, and confirmed that they had indeed succeeded.

Their exhaustion tempered their moment of triumph, but a renewed sense of purpose fueled them. With this precise code in hand, they were now one step closer to stopping the president's misuse of time travel.

He let out a sigh of relief. "*Finally*. Now, all we need is the opportunity."

Jesse nodded. "That's where we need to be careful. We can't afford to make any mistakes."

"We also have to consider the risks," she said. "What if we get caught?"

Silas nodded solemnly. "We'll need a foolproof plan and impeccable timing." He paused. "What was his name again?"

"William McDonald. He was part of the Boston facility that was doing what we were doing, but they couldn't figure out the right code. They were then attacked by the cult, which, funny enough, Control just happened to be the ones to rescue them."

"What a coincidence," Jesse said.

"I think capturing him the night we were here is the perfect moment," Silas said.

"I think you're right," Amelia said. "But if you're going to do this, you need to be very careful. You can't give yourself away. Study everything I printed out for you. It's not much, but it could make a difference."

"I think we need some sleep, and then tomorrow…" He checked the time on his computer. "Well, I guess today, Silas, you study, and Amelia and I will get The Machine ready. We should do this tomorrow night. What do you both think?"

They both agreed, so they all pulled out their cots that they had been napping on. They had been sleeping in the room because they hadn't been able to trust anyone.

Morning came quickly. They woke up as Jesse's wife, Sandra, walked into the room. She had brought them breakfast sandwiches and coffee. As much as she didn't care for Jesse being gone so many nights, she knew this was what he needed to do.

He got up and kissed his wife, but she pulled away.

"Honey, your breath," she said. "Please go brush your teeth. All of you." She looked the trio over. "Brush your teeth and shower. I washed some clothes for you; it's in my bag." She set the food and her bag on the table and handed them their clothes.

They ate and drank, and one by one, they went to get cleaned. Sandra cleaned up around the place and lit a candle because the room had become a little foul-smelling.

After all was said and done, they thanked Sandra, and Jesse kissed his wife again, now with minty fresh breath.

"Much better," she said, smiling. "Will you be home later?"

He sighed and kissed her cheek. "Probably not until much later. Tonight, we are trying something new, and I need to be here for at least the initial phase."

She nodded and kissed him once more. "We will be waiting for you when you get home."

They exchanged their expressions of love and goodbyes. She also bid farewell to Amelia and Silas, who responded in kind.

After Sandra's departure, the trio prepared for the night's operation. They reviewed their plan once more, ensuring every detail was accounted for. Silas spent hours studying the materials Amelia had gathered about William McDonald, while Jesse and she checked and rechecked the code to ensure it was perfect.

As the evening approached, the room's tension grew. They couldn't help but feel a sense of unease, knowing they were about to confront a shadowy figure within their own government.

Hours later, it was time to put their plan into action. Everything was set in place.

Jesse placed a reassuring hand on Silas's shoulder. "You've got this, Silas."

Amelia gave Silas a supportive nod.

He took a deep breath and nodded back. "I'll do my best."

Silas did as he had done before: he lay on the bed. They

strapped him in, attached the band to his head, and inserted the IV into his arm. They then wished him luck once again.

"Are you ready?" Jesse asked.

Silas nodded.

"Three. Two. One."

The world around him went black.

Light, colors, shapes, and voices rushed around Silas. All at once. His memory then snapped back to who he was and what he was doing. He now stood in the room next to the control room. He looked around and rubbed his eyes.

"William, are you okay?" a strange lady asked.

He didn't answer.

"William?" she asked again.

"Oh yes, I am," he said. "I'm fine. Must have moved too quickly or something."

"Oh, okay. Well, maybe you need to drink some water or get some fresh air."

He rubbed his eyes once more, suddenly aware that he needed to breathe. He had forgotten how strange it was to be in someone else's body. Simple tasks weren't as easy as they were on his own. At first, he had to manually control basic functions—like breathing.

"Yeah. I'll be all right," he replied, his voice sounding unfamiliar with a thick Boston accent.

He looked around. It seemed like they were sitting there organizing files, looking through the trio's notebooks and research and scanning documents.

"So, where are we on this?" he asked. "What else needs to be done?"

She looked a little puzzled. "Are you sure you're okay, Will?

You seem off."

He nodded. "Yeah, I'm good. Just tired. I think my brain ran out of juice," he said with a laugh.

She chuckled in return. "You were about to head to the room with the machine and take photos of everything. Apparently, the president wants us to take our time though, I heard. To see how these people turn out to trust him with their machine. Hopefully, they're not big enough fools, but I don't know."

"Yeah. Hopefully, they don't. But whatever. We are here doing a job, right?" He sighed. "Well, I'll go ahead and go take the pictures." But before he left the room, he remembered that he and Amelia were in the control room at that time. "I'm going to go to the bathroom first if anyone needs me."

She nodded and waved him off.

He left and peeked into the control room, seeing his past self and Amelia working quickly. It was weird looking at himself. Like looking at a mirror but not everything lined up.

He walked away, heading to the bathroom. In the bathroom, he nearly jumped, forgetting what he looked like in the mirror. After a few minutes of touching his face and trying to get himself back to reality, he poked his head out the door and saw his past self doing the same thing. His past self and Amelia then darted down the hallway and out the way they came in.

Silas—or William, as he wasn't sure what to call himself yet— took photos of the time travel machine, which led him to believe that the team's existing photos wouldn't be accurate since his past self had just taken some of the machine's parts.

He then returned to the other room with the lady, and they continued to work. A few hours later, they completed everything, gathered their equipment, and boarded buses to return to the hotel. He checked his wallet and found a room key with a number on it, which was fortunate.

Once they arrived at the hotel, a Control member stood at the front of the bus. "Listen here. Once off this bus, don't leave the hotel for any reason. Everything you need is provided here, and if you still need something, call the front desk, and we will get it. We'll pick you all up tomorrow."

They got off the bus and unloaded their personal equipment.

"Hey, William," the strange lady from before called. "We're headed to the bar in the lobby after we put up our stuff. Do you want to come?"

"Umm… Yeah, sure. After a day like this, why not?"

She smiled and walked away.

He went up to his room and set his wallet and phone down. Being still felt weird—like wearing someone else's used clothing that hadn't been washed. He looked through this person's luggage for anything and then checked his phone. Thankfully, it could be unlocked with his face. But nothing was out of the ordinary about this man. Other than the fact he liked to play cribbage.

After a quick freshening up, Silas—or William, as he decided to stick with for now—headed down to the lobby. He found the team at the bar, their faces showing signs of relief and exhaustion.

The strange lady from before greeted him with a friendly smile. "Glad you could make it," she said, motioning for him to join the group.

As they sat around the table, they ordered drinks and shared stories, attempting to find some semblance of normalcy in a situation that was anything but ordinary. William tried his best to fit in, mimicking their casual conversations and mannerisms.

"Hey, Will," one said. "Tell us something interesting about yourself."

William hesitated for a moment. "Well, I do enjoy a good game of cribbage."

The others chuckled.

"Cribbage, huh?" someone chimed in. "That's a unique choice. We'll have to play a round sometime."

Throughout the evening, William kept a close eye on his new colleagues, learning their habits, personalities, and quirks. He was adapting to his new identity, albeit temporarily, while keeping a watchful eye on his true mission: finding the information they needed to expose the president's sinister plans.

The next morning, he woke up with a bad migraine, realizing that William's body didn't possess his usual tolerance for alcohol. He got out of bed, showered, and dressed before heading down to the hotel's breakfast area. Breakfast consisted of the typical hotel fare. Some of his team members were already there, but they had no updates to share. He decided to return to his room, hoping to alleviate his headache.

There, he continued his search through William's phone, checking emails and text messages. Hours passed. A text message then arrived, notifying them that the buses would pick them up in two hours to take them to the airport for their return to DC. The facility's proximity to the president intrigued William.

He decided to head downstairs for lunch, which featured various sandwich options. He took his time, people-watching to stave off the boredom that had crept in during his hours alone.

As he observed people, he couldn't help but wonder about

these team members. Were they all aware of the president's true intentions? How deep did the deception run, or were there others who, like him, questioned the situation?

Trying to put his thoughts about the team aside, though they weren't technically his team but rather William's, he headed back to the room. He packed what William had brought along, and when the time came, he joined everyone downstairs.

The buses arrived right on schedule. They reached the airport in thirty minutes. However, instead of going to the typical drop-off terminal, they drove through another gate to the back, where a plane was waiting.

Within twenty minutes, they boarded, and the plane took off. As he sat in his seat by himself, he felt turbulence as the plane climbed into the air. The seatbelt sign turned off soon after. Then a presence stood next to him. Captain Joel.

"Hello, William. I need to talk to you," Captain Joel said.

William froze, taking a moment to remember that he still wasn't Silas. "Yes, of course, Captain Joel. Have a seat."

The captain sat in the row next to him. "So, I just wanted to bring it up to you that we will be setting this up for the president in a discreet location. We will have you and your crew in a nearby hotel again, but you all will have more freedom. The president is also going to want a briefing, so I was thinking that instead of me giving it and potentially messing it up, we could have him come by the facility to do it."

"That sounds great, Captain. Whatever makes all our jobs easier."

"Perfect. Now, remember our deal here. The NDA you all signed… Well, the pen wasn't the only thing that will come for you. If anything gets leaked, the person responsible for the leak will only be leaking blood." Captain Joel smiled.

William felt like cold water had just been poured down his back. "Yes, sir. I remember."

"Good!" The captain patted his shoulder, turned, and leaned back in his chair. "You should get some shut-eye while you can." He then closed his eyes and fell asleep.

William sat there, going over the conversation he had just had. Threatening these people... But was he much better? He had taken over this man's body, and the only way to get back was to do self-harm or knock himself out. Yet this was for the greater good, right?

He decided to not let it get to him and to take the captain's advice to rest. Who knew what awaited them when they'd land?

The plane shook as its wheels hit the landing strip. William woke up, wiped the gunk from his eyes, and looked out the window. The plane slowed and made its way toward the terminal, where a few vehicles were waiting for them.

The captain stood. "All right, everyone. Get off the plane and into those vehicles. We have people taking care of your bags. Let's hurry this up because we are on a time crunch."

They all got up, got off, and went into the vehicles. The windows were very tinted. So much so that he could barely see out.

"Where do you think they'll be taking us?" the strange lady from before asked—whose name he found out was Cindy as she got into the vehicle.

"All I know is that there is a facility with a hotel right next to it," he replied.

She had a look of concern in her eyes but shrugged it off.

And off they went. When the car stopped, William checked his cell phone. It had been about thirty minutes. The driver rolled the window down and handed a badge to someone outside. The gate lifted. A minute later, they came to another stop, and the driver told them to get out. The doors unlocked, and they slowly got out.

"All right, everyone," the captain said. "Welcome to your new facility. It's an old bread factory that we are repurposing. Go ahead and take a look around. There are plenty of boxes that still need unpacking and computers that still need to be set up. I have to meet with the president and update him. I want you to have this all set up by the time I get back. We have brought in outside help to assist you. I will be back in a few hours."

He got into a vehicle that sped off. Silas and the others went inside.

The captain wasn't wrong when he had said it had been an old bread factory. Rusted machines were on one side, and the walls were graffitied. A massive area had been emptied and was now filled with tables and boxes of computers.

They went to work, unboxing the computers, updating them, and setting them up for what they needed. They were all exhausted when the captain showed back up.

He walked up to William. "All right. How are we doing here? Is everything set up?"

William nodded. "Yes, sir."

"Good. Okay. For the machine, what do we need? Never mind. I don't care. What I need from y'all is to work on whatever it is you need to do and order parts. Select a handful to do the ordering and the others to do the nerd stuff. Don't purchase anything yet though. The president will be by tomorrow, and I want him to see this before we start buying anything."

William nodded again. "Um, yes, sir. I will get on it."

With a list of tasks assigned, the team got to work. William found himself in charge of coordinating the equipment and parts procurement. Although he knew everything there was to know about the time travel machine, he tried his best not to act like it. They used his photos and the documentation the Boston team stole to try and base the parts they needed.

As they scoured the internet for suppliers, he couldn't help but feel uneasy. He knew he had to do it, but it felt morally conflicting, knowing it was for the president.

Hours passed, and their efforts paid off. The facility had transformed into a makeshift headquarters.

The captain emerged from his office and addressed the exhausted team. "All right, everyone. I couldn't care less how long you all have to stay here. However, considering the president's desire for everything to work out correctly, I'll send half of you to get some sleep at the designated hotel. We'll swap in eight hours." He turned to William to decide who would take the first shift.

This wasn't as difficult for William as he had thought. Since he wasn't personally acquainted with anyone, he selected individuals at random from both teams. The rest then continued to work through the night and into the early morning.

Eventually, the time came to switch. Silas was walking with the crew to go to the hotel when a hand touched his shoulder. He turned.

"Hey, William," the captain said. "I need you here. The president will be arriving in an hour or two, and I need you to explain things to him that I cannot."

"Yes, sir," William replied, sounding exhausted.

The captain rolled his eyes. "Fine. Go sleep in one of the rooms over there. There should be a cot. I'll come get you when the president arrives."

William thanked him. In the room, he closed his eyes and fell asleep instantly. His dreams were strange, Silas's past mixed with William's. He didn't know if this was just from his exhaustion or if their pasts were intertwining.

A kick to the cot woke him up. Feeling like he had just fallen asleep, he looked up.

The captain towered over him. "Get up. Go rinse off your face and straighten up what you're wearing."

William nodded and did just that. As he walked out of the bathroom, he saw Jason talking with the captain. Reminding himself that the president didn't know he was Silas, he grabbed some documents and a checklist and caught up with them. They went into an office, where he gave the president the information he was told to. He handed over the documents, which the president ignored. After the president departed, the captain gave him the green light to start purchasing.

Over the next few days, they continued to build the machine and work on the coding. William snooped around, trying to find out as much as he could about the president's plan, but he didn't find much.

One day, the captain showed up, which wasn't out of the ordinary. He walked up to William and said, "William, the president would like to talk to you. Let's go."

William froze from fear, wondering why the president would want to meet with him. But he nodded and said, "Yes, sir." He handed his work over to Cindy, who had a concerned look on her face.

He followed the captain out to a vehicle, and this time, the captain drove. As they left the facility, he tried to memorize any landmarks or signs that might be useful for Amelia and

Jesse when he eventually returned.

They made several turns and got on the highway, speeding along. They continued down a few more streets and eventually arrived at a restaurant. Just like before, it was empty.

"Go inside," the captain said. "He's waiting for you."

William got out of the vehicle and made his way to the door. He opened it to find the president sitting at a booth a few rows back on the right. He slowly walked to the booth and sat.

The president's piercing eyes seemed to look right through him, making William feel like the president knew he wasn't actually William.

"I hope it's okay, but I went ahead and ordered for you," the president said with a smile. "Don't worry. I know exactly what you like. Gotta love technology. It remembers everything you do, what you say, and who you talk to."

"Thank you, sir."

"You see, the thing about me is that I know everything while others believe I know nothing. For instance, I know you were born in Boston Mass Gen Hospital, you're forty-two years old, and your parents stayed married until the untimely death of your mother, due to cancer. Your dad drank himself into a coma and gave up caring for his two sons. You were only what? Twelve?

"Your brother joined the military. How thoughtful. Why did he join? Hmm? Couldn't take Daddy's beatings anymore? But you stuck around. How interesting.

"Fast-forward ten years: your brother gets married after five deployments. That last one was a stinger, wasn't it? Lost an arm and most of his right leg. How long before depression kicked in? How long until he tried ending his life? I would guess not long. I wouldn't want to sit around while my wife decided she couldn't stand the sight of me anymore and left with my daughter. Ouch. He then turns to the bottle—just like your father. Then one day he's out of booze, money, and care and decides to end his life. But here's the thing, William: he failed at that too. What a shame. Now he has horrendous scarring on his face and is completely paralyzed, living the last of his days in a home."

The shock of everything the president said hit Silas, leaving him frozen in his seat.

The waitress brought the food to the table, he looked down at it and it was chicken fried steak. It was William's favorite dish.

"With all that trauma, you stuck around with your dad but not for your war hero of a brother. What a shame," the president continued. "Oh, don't give me that look. I know you feel terrible, and I'm sure you tried everything you could. But things happen, right?

"I'm not here to tell you how awful of a brother you are, what your credit score is, who you've slept with in the last ten years, or even how, as you sit here now, your wife—well, I'm assuming after this, your ex-wife—is sleeping with your neighbor. What I'm here for isn't a warning or anything. I'm here to help you.

"What if I can help you? Think about being able to stop your brother from going on that last deployment. Think about going into the future to find the cure for cancer and then bringing it to your mom. Think about going back and being there for your wife more, so she wouldn't have to find love next door?"

The president paused to take a bite of his burger.

William sat there, his mind racing as he contemplated the

horrifying experiences the man he had taken over had endured. The president was now offering him a chance at a better life, but William couldn't shake the feeling that there was a hidden agenda at play.

"That sounds wonderful," William responded. "But why choose me, sir?"

The president briefly paused to savor his meal, washing it down with a sip of cola. "The thing is, Will… Or do you prefer William? It doesn't matter." He smirked. "The point, Will, is that I need you to ensure this operation goes flawlessly. I have plans that will reshape the world as we know it. I won't claim it's for the betterment of the world but rather for the betterment of this country, particularly my own life.

"You might be wondering if I want to use the machine to save my mother or something sentimental like that. But no. I enjoyed a normal, happy childhood and have a beautiful wife and three daughters… Well, two now. Anyway, what I truly desire is more power, and that can only happen once I'm certain this machine works. Once it does, I can achieve whatever I want. And if you work alongside me, I'll do my best to help resolve your issues."

William remained in a state of shock.

"So, will the machine be ready?" the president inquired. "Do you trust your team to have it operational?"

"Yes. They're all highly capable. They're currently assembling the machine even without my presence."

The president nodded. "Excellent. I'm pleased we had this discussion. Since your team is self-sufficient, and you've had a moment to relax, let's proceed." He gestured for William to enjoy his meal.

As William began eating, an abrupt explosion rocked the

room, causing his eardrums to throb. Darkness overtook his vision. His body collapsed face-first into his plate.

Chaos erupted from the kitchen area, the chef and waitstaff screaming in terror.

"I'm relieved to have finally shared my true intentions," the president calmly remarked. "I couldn't risk him revealing anything to anyone."

Swiftly, the president wiped the gun of any fingerprints and placed it in William's lifeless hand.

Captain Joel entered the scene and turned to the president. "I'll take care of the situation inside. The screaming is becoming quite bothersome."

The captain entered the back area, where screams echoed before three gunshots rang out. The chaos silenced.

Meanwhile, the president rose from his seat, completed his soda, and exited the restaurant.

Captain Joel reached behind the grill and broke the gas hose, which emitted a hiss. He then ignited a wad of paper near the front entrance before getting into the vehicle and driving away with the president.

In the rearview mirror, the president witnessed the restaurant explode.

The Fourteenth Chapter: Unveiling Chaos

The sound of a pistol firing repeated in Silas's ears, his eardrums exploding. The sensation of the bullet piercing through his forehead. Cracking his skull. Then darkness.

Was this death?

He then commanded himself to breathe and open his eyes, yelling at himself internally. A bursting sound happened again like a thunderclap splitting the silence, and he sat up, gasping for air, feeling his body, and realizing his head was still intact.

"You look like you've seen a monster," Jesse said.

Silas's eyes finally caught his surroundings. He saw Jesse and Amelia, the latter looking worried. "Water."

She handed him her bottle of water.

He chugged it and wiped away the water from the sides of his mouth and chin. "We were right. I know where it is."

She and Jesse exchanged glances, their expressions a mix of anticipation and concern. Silas's mind raced with newfound determination as he explained what he had seen and experienced. He recounted the president's cryptic words, described the president's obsession with power, and emphasized the urgency of the situation.

As he spoke, the gravity of their mission weighed on all

three of them. They knew they had to act quickly, but they also understood the risks. The president was a formidable adversary, and they were just a small group of scientists with limited resources.

Amelia, her analytical mind working in overdrive, formulated a plan. "We need concrete evidence," she said. "Something that will expose the president's true intentions and make it impossible for him to carry out his plans."

Jesse nodded. "And we'll need allies. People who can help us take on the president and his supporters."

Silas knew they were right. They couldn't afford to back down now. "I don't think exposing him to the people or media is going to achieve anything. I believe Jesse is right, but I think we need to shut down the facility.

"Our mission isn't merely a personal endeavor." His voice resonated with deeper conviction. "It's a quest to safeguard the fabric of time. The president's intentions pose a grave threat not only to our lives but to the future of humanity."

Amelia nodded solemnly. "We must act decisively and strategically. Our responsibility goes beyond exposing his actions; we need to prevent him from achieving his goals."

"The three of us can't do this on our own though," Jesse said. "Who could we enlist to stop him?"

They sat and pondered this question, realizing it wasn't a simple one to answer. They brainstormed some ideas, but the more they brainstormed, the harder it became to think of a solution.

"Well, what if we used a group who doesn't like us but really hates the president?" Amelia asked. "The one group the president has abused lately?"

Silas and Jesse looked at each other and then back at Amelia.

"You couldn't mean…" Jesse said.

"The Cult of the Sacred Bodies?" Silas said. "Them? They really don't like us, Amelia."

"But they really *hate* the president," she said. "He's been killing them and poisoning the minds of this country with false news about their protests." She leaned forward, her eyes filled with determination. "I know it's a long shot, but desperate times call for desperate measures. Besides, they have a strong network, resources, and we can suspect a burning desire for revenge. If we can convince them that our goal aligns with theirs, they might be willing to help."

Silas nodded slowly, considering the idea. "It's risky, but it might be our best shot. Let's see if we can make contact with someone from their organization and gauge their interest."

Jesse, still a bit skeptical, said, "All right. We'll give it a try. But we have to be cautious and make sure we're not falling into some trap. And where would we even start? How would we find their leader?"

"I might be able to help you with that," a familiar voice called from the doorway.

They turned. It was Sandra, Jesse's wife.

"What do you mean?" he asked.

"Sally's friends' mom is in the group. I see her at PTA meetings every now and then. If anything, we can go to her and ask," Sandra said.

Silas looked at all of them and then back at Sandra. "Sandra, that might be the breakthrough we need."

"NO!" Jesse snapped. "I won't let my family get involved in this. I just…can't. It's too risky."

"Come on, Jesse," Sandra pleaded. "She's a wonderful lady, and they mean no harm. All I'll do is talk to her this Friday at the next PTA meeting. You all can sit in the parking lot or whatever. Just write a letter. I can hand that to her and try to explain why I need her to deliver it to whoever is in charge. The worst thing that can happen is she says no."

Silas, Amelia, and Jesse exchanged glances, weighing the risks and potential benefits of involving Sandra in their mission.

After a brief silence, Silas spoke first. "Sandra, we appreciate your willingness to help, but we also understand Jesse's concerns. It's crucial to prioritize the safety of your family."

Amelia nodded. "We'll prepare the letter, and if you feel comfortable going ahead, we'll support you in every step of the way. But if at any point you sense danger or change your mind, please don't hesitate to step back."

Jesse, still hesitant, sighed. "All right. But only if you promise to be cautious, Sandra. Your safety comes first."

She smiled and nodded, relieved that they had reached an understanding. "Thank you. All of you. I'll do my best to make sure nothing bad happens."

And so the plan was set.

For the next three days, they worked on the letter and strategized how to stop the president, both with and without the cult's possible help.

Yet once, while watching the news, the anchor said, "In memory we look back to when William McDonald and the staff of a local eatery in Washington DC were found in a burned-down building. It appears that William shot the staff and set fire to the restaurant before taking his own life."

Silas looked at Jesse and Amelia, a mix of shock and amusement on his face.

"So, you're a murderer," Jesse said sarcastically, laughing at the absurd story.

"Well, I guess we can add mass murderer to your list of accomplishments, Silas," she added. She couldn't help but find the whole situation so ridiculous that it was almost comical.

Silas chuckled. "I do feel bad for William though. He didn't deserve that, but there was nothing I could do. It was meant to happen."

Jesse nodded. "Okay. Tomorrow is Friday. We need to get moving. Amelia, do you have the letter?"

She nodded.

"Perfect. I'll give it to Sandra for her to take to the meeting. I'll come pick you two up from your apartment, Silas. Is it cleaned up?"

"Yes," Silas replied. "They finished the mess and the investigation the other day."

"All right. The PTA meeting is at ten a.m. I'll pick you two up at 9:15. Let's call it a night, and I'll see y'all then."

They all agreed, hoping their plan would unfold smoothly.

As they prepared to disperse for the night, Silas couldn't help but feel a sense of nervous anticipation.

Amelia could read his expression and gave him an encouraging smile. "We've come this far, Silas. We can do this."

He nodded. "You're right. We have to."

They headed to the parking garage, and Jesse bid his goodbyes to them. On the way to his apartment, they made a quick stop to grab some food and liquor. They ate, drank, showered, drank some more, and eventually fell asleep.

The following day, they both woke up and got ready for the day. They both drank some coffee and ate the leftover fried rice. He fried a few eggs and added them on top of the rice. It wasn't much, but it was something.

Silas's phone buzzed. Jesse was pulling up.

He and Amelia grabbed their stuff and walked down to the front. Jesse pulled up as they walked out the door, and they got in. The school was about fifteen minutes away. Jesse decided to use that time to talk about what he, Sandra, and Sally did last night, which ended up being just watching a movie and making silly popcorn, which was just fresh popcorn with colored food dye. Something his daughter loved.

But as they approached the school, the nervous tension in the car grew.

Ten minutes later, Sandra pulled up and parked a row down from where they were. She noticed their presence but avoided making eye contact. At 9:50, she got out of her car and walked toward the school. More parents were arriving and heading inside.

A buzz from Jesse's phone caught his attention. "That's her. The one in the green," he said, relaying Sandra's message.

They spotted a woman in a green dress making her way toward the school.

For the next forty-five minutes, they sat and waited. Sandra provided updates on her boredom during the meeting and shared that the woman they needed was sitting next to her. They appeared to have engaged in a conversation about a new casserole recipe.

As the meeting concluded, parents started leaving one by one. Sandra and the woman in green eventually emerged. The trio couldn't overhear their conversation nor could discern anything from Sandra's expression. She handed the woman in green the note, and the woman in green nodded before walking away. Sandra returned to her car and got in.

Another buzz from Jesse's phone. He summarized the message aloud. "Sandra said the woman was wonderful. She expressed interest in meeting with us and wants to bring one of the local leaders, who will then arrange a meeting with the family leader. She even included laughing emojis. The woman will text Sandra with a time and place to meet."

Excitement and relief washed over the trio. It seemed their efforts were paying off.

Jesse drove them back to Silas's apartment with renewed determination. "We are going to have to plan our discussion. This is essentially a sales pitch to them."

Amelia and Silas agreed.

As they pulled up, he received a text from Sandra. "She will have you three over at her house on Monday at nine a.m. She will provide snacks and drinks. Don't be late."

He shared the message with the other two, and they all looked at each other. That was in three days.

"You two enjoy your afternoon, come over for dinner, and bring stuff to sleep in," Jesse said. "You can stay in our guest bedroom. This way, we can work this out."

They both agreed and got out of the car.

They spent the rest of the day relaxing and packing a small backpack each. When it was time to head over to Jesse's house, they drove over, arriving early. Jesse's family greeted them.

They set their stuff down in the guest room and then went into the living room, where Jesse was playing Go Fish with his daughter. Sally invited them to join, and they couldn't refuse. Afterward, they enjoyed a wonderful home-cooked meal.

When Sally went off to bed, they started planning, intending to spend a good amount of time that night and the following day working on questions and concerns they had regarding the president. They aimed to align their issues with what the president was doing to show the cult that they were not so different when it came to their hatred toward the president. They found it refreshing to work outside of the facility, and Sandra popped in here and there to give her input or help. On Sunday, they finalized their presentation.

As the final day came to an end, they enjoyed their last dinner before the meeting. It was filled with laughs and old stories. After cleaning up, they gathered in the living room. Jesse brought out the whiskey and poured drinks for the adults. They talked about family, college, and the future, while Sally fell asleep on Sandra's lap.

Jesse looked at the clock, noticing it was getting late. "All right. It's time for bed. We need to be well-rested. I'll knock on your door when it's time to get up."

Silas and Amelia nodded. They got up, put their cups in the sink, and went off to bed. They fell asleep quite quickly, probably due to the whiskey.

That next morning, Jesse pounded on the door.

It was time.

The Fifteenth Chapter: Meeting Among Sacred

Silas, Jesse, and Amelia left Jesse's house, and off they went. They had discovered that the woman in green's name was Katherine, and her house was only about thirty minutes away.

"How are you feeling about this?" Silas asked Jesse.

"I feel pretty good," Jesse replied.

But as they drove closer to her house, the tension in the car mounted. Silas couldn't help but feel a mix of nervousness and excitement. He glanced at Amelia, who appeared more resolute. Her determination was evident in her expression.

The neighborhood gradually transformed, becoming quieter and more secluded. Katherine's house was an elegant two-story structure, surrounded by lush greenery and tall oak trees. It looked like the home of a person who held some influence.

Jesse parked the car, and they all took a deep breath before stepping out. With their hearts pounding, they walked up to Katherine's front door.

Jesse rang the doorbell, and a few seconds later, he saw someone approach through the door's frosted window. The door swung open, revealing Katherine in an elegant floor-length emerald green dress, adorned with a beautiful emerald and sapphire necklace that resembled a flower.

"Welcome, my beautiful people," she greeted them.

They entered her magnificent house. Its dark marble floors and staircase that faded upward gave it an almost ethereal quality. A grand chandelier hung in the entrance, and to the right sat a beautiful piano.

"Please take off your shoes," she said. "The maids just left, and I would rather not have the floor scuffed or dirt tracked in."

They complied, and she directed them to a room on the left, asking them to sit on the white couches, which looked pristine and seemed untouched. Which also made Silas nervous about sitting on them.

Katherine settled on the opposite couch as they took their seats. "Now, before we get into the dirty business, would you all like something to drink or eat?" she inquired, snapping her fingers.

The door behind her swung open, and three individuals entered, carrying silver platters.

"We have coffee, tea, and snacks."

The three attendants placed the offerings on the coffee table in front of them. Katherine poured herself a cup of green tea and selected a small sandwich. They followed suit, partaking in the refreshments.

As they sipped their drinks and nibbled on their snacks, they engaged in some small talk. Katherine maintained a polite and poised demeanor before finally addressing the elephant in the room.

"I assume you didn't come here for leisurely tea and snacks though," she said. "Tell me what brings you to my doorstep."

Silas, Jesse, and Amelia exchanged a quick glance, silently deciding who would take the lead in explaining their purpose.

Silas, being the most articulate, cleared his throat. "First of all, thank you for opening your house to us. It is as beautiful and elegant as you are.

"We are here to discuss a common enemy—the president. We understand you and your group may have some reservations about us due to our past actions. We acknowledge that we played a part in this issue with him. Our machine was initially intended for benevolent purposes, but his actions have forced us to reevaluate our stance. He has not only attacked us but copied all our work. He is exploiting this technology to gain control over the world."

Katherine sat there for a few moments, taking in their words. "First, thank you for your kind words. Second, you three are not just partly responsible for this situation; you are the reason he has acquired this power. So, don't assume I'm naive. And don't apologize insincerely because I can see it on your faces. Now, what precisely do you want from us?"

"We would like your help in stopping him from continuing these actions," Amelia said. "We've located the machine he has set up, but we cannot accomplish this on our own. We understand that we have differing beliefs, but if you all are willing to temporarily set those aside, we can prevent the president from causing further harm and find a way to foster understanding and peace between our respective groups."

Katherine took a moment to contemplate what Amelia had just said. She took a sip of her tea and leaned back, her gaze studying the three of them. After a brief silence, she finally spoke, her voice measured. "Your proposition is intriguing, and it's true that the president's actions have become increasingly concerning. However, I must consult with our leader. She is ultimately the one who makes the decisions for the cult, as you call us, but we consider ourselves more of a following."

Silas, Jesse, and Amelia exchanged looks.

"I will arrange a meeting between you and our leader, but I must warn you that she is a woman of strong convictions. Convincing her will not be an easy task. But I will convey what you have passed onto me."

Jesse nodded. "We understand. We're willing to do whatever it takes. Please arrange the meeting as soon as possible. Time is of the essence."

She looked at him. "I know that. You don't have to tell me."

"Yes, ma'am."

"I'll go ahead and make the call," she said.

A butler walked in with a rotary phone. It was beautifully adorned with a gold and white floral design, but Silas couldn't help but think it was a bit of an overkill.

The phone call was short, and they couldn't hear the other end. Katherine kept responding with quick, one- or two-word answers. She hung up with a smile.

"She can meet you tomorrow," she said. "I'll write down the time and place for you."

She looked over at the butler and asked for a pen and paper. He left with the phone and returned with both. She wrote down the address and time and then handed it to Silas.

A thud and a scream came from the kitchen. They all rushed into the kitchen and found the butler bleeding out on the floor, clutching a bloody knife in his hand. Jesse flipped him over and saw that his neck had been sliced.

"WHAT THE HELL?!" Katherine screamed. "WHY?!"

Jesse, Silas, and Amelia exchanged fearful glances.

"He succeeded," Silas said.

"What?!" she replied, tears streaming down her face.

"He completed building the machine," Jesse explained. "The only way to return from time traveling is by becoming unconscious or, well, taking your own life."

She, still confused, continued to weep over her butler.

"But why was he here?" Amelia asked. "How did he know?"

Silas recalled his previous experience inside William's body. "He knows everything. He must've been listening to us through our phones or watching us via street cameras or something." He then grabbed his phone and threw it onto the ground, breaking it. He took out the SIM card and destroyed it.

The others followed suit, destroying their phones as well.

Katherine turned toward them, makeup running down her face. Blood now stained her green dress. She got up, grabbed a piece of paper, and wrote down a new address, which she handed to Silas. The paper had blood smeared on it from her hands.

"Take this. Go here now. Don't go home," she said. "Jesse, I'll get in contact with Sandra and inform her. Do you know where this is?"

He glanced at the address. "I think so. I have a map in my car."

"I will reach out to our leader after you all leave. I will let her know in code if he is still listening. But please, go now. Time is essential."

Silas looked at her. "I am sorry. We didn't mean—"

"Just go! Stop him from doing this again!"

The situation propelled them into action.

Silas, Jesse, and Amelia hastily left Katherine's home. As they hurried toward Jesse's car, she couldn't help but feel a gnawing sense of vulnerability. Their enemy—the president—was now privy to their every move, and she had no idea how deeply he could penetrate their plans.

Jesse navigated them through the Dallas streets, heading toward the new address Katherine had provided—which was in Hot Springs, Arkansas.

Silas kept glancing out the rearview mirror, half expecting to see government agents or mysterious figures tailing them.

Amelia broke the silence, her voice slightly trembling. "Do you think the leader can help us? What if she wants nothing to do with us?"

"We don't really have a choice now," Jesse said.

They continued on I-30 E, making various stops. Silas and Amelia had the good idea to withdraw as much cash as they could in case the president tried freezing their accounts. Jesse checked his account, and it looked like Sandra might have done the same.

At one of the stops, Jesse found an old payphone with who knew what germs on it and called Sandra to discreetly let her know how they were. He couldn't talk for long.

As they continued their journey, the tension inside the car was palpable. The knowledge that the president could be listening to their every word unsettled them.

Silas couldn't help but replay the tragic events that had unfolded at Katherine's house in his mind. The butler's lifeless gaze haunted him, and he couldn't shake the guilt for involving Katherine and her staff in their dangerous mission.

Jesse's grip on the steering wheel tightened as they approached Hot Springs. The city, known for its natural hot springs and historic bathhouses, seemed like an unusual place for such a clandestine meeting. He wondered if the Cult of the Sacred Bodies had chosen this location deliberately to avoid drawing attention.

"We should be cautious when we arrive," Amelia said. "We don't know what kind of reception awaits us, and we certainly don't want to tip off the president."

Jesse nodded, his eyes fixed on the road. "We'll need to approach with utmost care. Our next steps are crucial."

They approached a gate, a simple metal one that they might find on a farm or rural property. Devoid of any signs or markers. A man stood nearby.

Jesse rolled down his window. "Hello. We're here to meet with the leader. I'm Jesse, and this is Amelia and Silas."

"She's waiting for you," the man at the gate replied and proceeded to open the gate.

He rolled up the window and drove through, entering a long, bumpy dirt driveway that led to an aged and weathered white house that had a yellow hue from time and dust. The paint had faded, and the wooden boards showed signs of cracking from the passage of time and the forces of nature.

Amelia couldn't help but comment, "So much for the stereotypical cultlike compound. I was expecting something different."

Jesse parked the vehicle and turned off the ignition. As they all stepped out, a woman emerged from the house and descended the porch stairs. She had short, shoulder-length brown hair that framed her face elegantly, a sharp chin, and piercing dark blue eyes. Her attire consisted of a green and brown flannel shirt, ripped dark jeans, and sturdy hiking boots.

She spoke as she approached them. "You must be Jesse, Amelia, and Silas. I've heard quite a bit about you three. It's unfortunate about Katherine's butler; he was a good man." She extended her hand. "I'm the leader of the so-called cult. My name is Scarlet."

She stood there, studying them intently. Her gaze seemed to delve into their pasts and present as if they were open books. "Well, let's go inside and have a little chat."

The Sixteenth Chapter: Scarlet's Gambit

The trio entered the house behind Scarlet. After going down a hallway, she led them into what looked like a living room, but it had several tables covered with maps and papers strewn about. A few chairs were in the corner, which they grabbed and moved over to the table to sit on.

"So, why us, hmm?" Scarlet asked. "Why the one group that does not like what you're doing? Why come to us for help?"

Silas exchanged a glance with Jesse and Amelia, contemplating how best to explain their predicament. "We understand there are differences in our beliefs and methods," he said, choosing his words carefully. "But the president's actions go far beyond our ideological differences. He's exploiting the time machine for his own gain and threatening the very fabric of our world."

"Our goal is to stop him from using the machine for his personal advantage," Jesse added. "He already has it set up, and he used it as a threat at Katherine's house. We believe that despite our differences, we can find common ground in the fight against a common enemy."

They continued to talk about Jason's machine, what Silas saw through William's eyes, and shared insights about the future based on Silas's experiences.

Scarlet listened, her piercing gaze unwavering. After a moment of silence, she slowly nodded, acknowledging the gravity of the situation. "I'll be honest with you: our beliefs have led us on a different path. But it seems our paths might have become parallel, leading to the same destination."

Silas was about to speak, but she cut him off.

"Listen, I don't need you to give me your sad puppy eyes and beg on your knees."

Her words frustrated Amelia. He put his hand on her knee to calm her.

"Hmm," Scarlet said. "We have a lover boy here. How cute. But here's the thing: I run a following, and you need my help. Not the other way around. I've listened to your story. My question is: how are we going to stop someone who can already see the future with his own machine?"

"Well, the thing is," Jesse said, "that we've recently concluded that with time travel, the future can always change due to the present. It hasn't been written in the time line yet, which is what he's trying to do.

"So, for example, if he goes into the future for a week, sees himself getting into a fender bender, and then comes back, he can just not go driving that day. The fender will never happen. But if he remembers a flat he got five years ago and would like that to not affect his present, no matter what he does, he cannot prevent himself from getting the flat. Even if he kills the battery in his car, it will always end with him getting that flat. For some reason, time stops him from doing it. Or it will get corrected somehow."

After she took that in, she said, "So why hasn't he tried taking over your bodies?" She pointed at the trio.

He leaned forward. "We're not entirely sure why. We don't know if it has anything to do with Silas's previous time travel experience or if he simply doesn't care to. Maybe he has a bigger purpose for us. We just don't know. But as long as he doesn't know where we are or who we are with, we don't think he can get to us."

Her brow furrowed as she pondered his words. "So, not a whole lot of understanding about something you built."

"Well, we don't know if anyone will ever understand—"

"Here's the thing: if we are going to do this, we need to do it under the radar. We can't be using any form of the internet until we take down Jasons machine."

The trio agreed with her.

"There is one thing I do want if we do this. I would like to look him in the eyes while the machine gets destroyed."

The trio looked at each other, confused.

"Why?" Amelia asked.

Scarlet looked at her. "Jason King is my father. My name is Scarlet King."

A hushed silence fell upon the room as the weight of her revelation settled in. Silas, Jesse, and Amelia exchanged stunned looks. The realization that they were sitting in the presence of Jason King's daughter—the very man they sought to thwart—sent shivers down their spines.

Scarlet continued, her voice tinged with a mix of frustration and determination. "I grew up under his shadow. Even before the twins, I wasn't loved as a daughter. He was always about power. Mother never saw it either; she was either ignorant or didn't care. The hatred he showed toward me was because I wasn't always ladylike. I wasn't the *perfect* daughter for the soon-to-be president, as he always called himself.

"Then he had the twins, who became his pride and joy. He trained them to be in the public eye from a very young age. He kept me out of any press pictures. Most of the time, they would just leave me at home. He never saw it for how it was. He hated me, but he would never admit that."

She sighed and took a sip of water. "I couldn't take it anymore. I ran away. They say they tried to look for me, but he couldn't care less. Mother tried to reach out a few times, but I couldn't face either of them anymore. I was on my own for a while, and then I found people like me. Broken and hurt. We healed each other.

"Then people like you popped up—facilities claiming to build time travel machines, trying to fix the world when it can't be fixed. Changing the future shouldn't be *easy*. Things need to happen, so people can learn and grow rather than cheating life. So, we gathered individuals with the same beliefs, and we grew quite rapidly. Sadly, with any group, we have our delinquents, but we try to get rid of them before they can do too much damage. We also are aware of the false attacks on your facility and others. The worst we do is block the driveway to your parking lot. We aren't here to harm people."

Silas finally found his voice amid the emotional storm that had unfolded in her revelation. "Your perspective is enlightening, Scarlet. We would have never thought you are the president's daughter. Nor did I know he *had* a third daughter. But let's stand united in the pursuit of a common goal—to prevent the president from misusing the time machine for his own personal gain."

Amelia nodded. "We're ready to work together, Scarlet, if you are."

Scarlet offered a faint smile, appreciative of their willingness to collaborate. "Good. Now, let's focus on how we can bring down the machine and stop the president's plans. We'll need a meticulous plan, one that leaves no room for error."

The room filled with a renewed sense of purpose, and the unlikely alliance between the three researchers and the Cult of the Sacred Bodies took shape.

Scarlet stood and called one of her people over. "Take these three to two rooms upstairs to rest. They look like they need it, and it's getting late." She then addressed the trio. "We will send something up to eat. And in the morning, we will plan, so rest up." She shooed them away.

Upstairs in their room, Silas and Amelia noticed a set of clothes for both of them. They weren't too fancy. Just jeans and a green shirt for him and jeans and a long-sleeved green shirt for her. They looked at each other.

"I guess green is their color," Amelia said.

After freshening up and changing into the provided sleep-wear that was in one of the drawers, Silas and Amelia settled into their room. The dimly lit space had a cozy feel to it, and despite the strange circumstances, they both appreciated the chance to rest.

A knock sounded at the door, and a member brought them food, consisting of basic sandwiches and orange soda. They sat at the edge of the bed and ate, enjoying each other's company.

When another knock came, it was Jesse. "Hey, you two. I'm just checking in. This is wild, right? Like who would've thought?"

They both nodded.

"Well, I'm going to go eat and head to bed. I'm *exhausted*. They said they would let me call Sandra in the morning from a burner phone. I'll see y'all then." He then left.

They finished their meal and set the plates on the dresser.

As they sat on the bed, she turned to Silas, her eyes reflecting a mix of curiosity and concern. "Silas, can you believe all of this? That Scarlet is the president's daughter? That we're working with her… It's surreal."

He nodded, his mind still trying to process everything. "I know. It's a lot to take in. But if we want to stop the president and protect the time machine, it seems like we don't have a choice."

She sighed, leaning back against the pillows. "I just hope we can trust her and her group. This whole situation feels like a gamble."

He placed a reassuring hand on her shoulder. "We'll have to be cautious, but for now, let's get some rest."

As they lay there, they held each other close, kissed each other, and drifted off to sleep. Their breathing gradually synchronized as they settled into a peaceful slumber.

The morning sun filtered through the window, casting streaks of light through the blinds. A rhythmic knock echoed through the room, rousing Silas and Amelia from their slumber.

"Hey, it's time to get up," a voice from beyond the door said. "Be downstairs in fifteen minutes."

They dressed in the clothes that were provided to them and made their way downstairs.

Scarlet was already in the living room, engrossed in the maps spread out before her. She was sketching out plans for the journey to DC. "Good morning, you two. Grab a breakfast taco from the kitchen. It may not be as good as what you have in Texas, but it's sustenance."

Following her advice, they entered the kitchen, each taking

two tacos and pouring themselves some orange juice. After returning to the living room, they joined Scarlet in examining the maps.

"Our route to DC needs to be discreet," she explained, "avoiding any government scrutiny or tracking. We'll have to travel by road, making strategic stops to rest and refuel along the way."

Silas and Amelia nodded.

"What about surveillance?" he asked, his eyes darting between the marked primary and secondary routes on the map. "How do we ensure we're not being tracked or followed?"

Deep in thought, Scarlet tapped her fingers on the table. "We'll need to assume they have eyes everywhere, so we should avoid major highways and stick to the back roads. We'll also change vehicles periodically to throw off anyone trying to tail us. And, of course, no phones or any electronic devices that can be traced."

Jesse joined the group, fresh from his conversation with his wife. "I talked to Sandra. I didn't tell her much. Just that I'm okay. She's gone to live with her sister."

She nodded. "I've gotten in contact with our Arlington group near DC. They said that they would have enough people and could meet us in DC when the time is ready."

"Good. That'll be amazing."

As they delved deeper into their strategy, urgency hung in the air. The fate of the world and the power of time itself rested in their hands.

"What will we do about Control?" Silas asked.

They all sat and pondered that question.

"Well, they aren't invincible," Scarlet said. "I mean, we could always bomb the place, right?"

"Bomb the place?!" Amelia exclaimed. "There are innocent people in there!"

"Then what idea do you have, sugar?"

She tried to think. "Well, I mean, we could try going at night. And defend ourselves against those who try to attack us."

"Amelia has a point," Silas said. "We should prioritize the safety of innocent civilians. If we can manage a covert operation during the night and avoid unnecessary harm, it's the ethical choice."

Scarlet leaned back, her gaze fixed on the map. "All right. We'll plan for a nighttime infiltration. But we need a distraction to divert their attention while we sneak in."

"What if we stage a protest outside the facility?" Jesse offered. "It would attract media attention and Control, giving us a chance to slip inside unnoticed."

She nodded. "That could work. We'll need to coordinate with our allies in DC for that. But it should be enough to draw Control away from the facility. And we'll have to be quick and efficient to get inside without any unnecessary confrontations."

"Will you be with us?" Jesse asked.

"No. I plan on standing in front of Jason during the attack."

"How?" Silas said. "How will you get into one of the highest secured buildings in the United States?"

Scarlet leaned back in her chair, her expression serious. "I have some contacts on the inside. People who still care about me. They'll provide me with the access I need."

Silas, Jesse, and Amelia exchanged looks, their curiosity piqued.

"You have contacts in the White House?" Silas asked. "But how?"

Scarlet looked at him. "Not everyone who works for my dad

necessarily agrees with him. Of course I've got someone on the inside. Little does he know, his secretary despises him." She chuckled. "She will get me in. I'll pretend I'm your typical tourist; he won't recognize me anyway. Once I'm in, she will find me and put me in her office. He never goes in there anyway. Then once he's done for the day, I'll visit him, which should be about the time you all get into the facility."

The group nodded, their skepticism slowly giving way.

"What happens if he refuses to meet with you?" Jesse asked.

"He won't," she replied confidently, "because I'll be visiting my sisters and mother at the same time. There's no refusing me and no ignoring me anymore."

"What will you do or say to him?" Silas pressed.

She shot him a stern look. "Well, that's not for you to worry about, is it? Your only concern is destroying the machine and any documentation they have."

The trio didn't question it any further.

As the day wore on, their plan took shape. They marked potential safe houses along the route, identified potential fuel stops, and planned when to switch vehicles. They left nothing to chance.

Scarlet's contacts in the White House provided critical information about her father's schedule and the layout of the building, allowing her to plan her approach with precision.

Amelia and Silas also worked on gathering supplies for their journey, including communication devices that couldn't be traced. Jesse coordinated with the Arlington team, ensuring they were ready to provide backup when needed.

As the evening approached, the four of them gathered around a table covered with maps and equipment. They knew the next few days would be fraught with danger and uncertainty, but they were prepared to do whatever it took to protect the future.

145

The Seventeenth Chapter: Through the Beast's Eyes

"How much longer do I have to wait?" the president said in the former bread factory. He grabbed a clipboard that was sitting on a desk next to him and threw it, hitting and cutting a young woman's face.

She dared not to move out of fear of the president.

He paced back and forth. "WELL?!"

Cindy stepped forward. "Well, sir, we are almost done. There was an issue in finding a certain part, but we found it. It should be here tomorrow, and by tomorrow evening, we should be good to go."

His face, which had been beet red, returned to its normal color. "That is all I ask. For someone to answer my damn question." He looked at the woman with the bleeding cut on her face. "You should really get that cleaned up. Nobody wants to see a woman like that. Hideous."

He then walked out and got into his vehicle. "Drive."

His driver drove them back to the White House. He sat there, his anger at why he couldn't have what he wanted right then swirling.

His mind raced with thoughts of the machine. The power it offered was intoxicating, and he couldn't wait to wield it.

Upon arriving, he wasted no time. He went straight to his office, ignoring his family and his secretary. There, he sat and planned. Eventually, Joel called.

"Hey, Jason," he said. "I just wanted to let you know that I think the trio are up to something. Ever since the incident with Torres, I've been following them through all the camera feeds. Something is off."

Jason took in his words. "Well, keep an eye on them. I'll give you permission to use their phones and listen in on their conversations. Let me know if there is anything."

"Sounds good. I will."

As he hung up, a sinister smile crept across his face. He had always been one step ahead of his adversaries, and this situation was no different. He relished the idea of having an edge, especially when it came to Silas, Jesse, and Amelia. They were becoming a thorn in his side, and he was determined to take them out once and for all.

He pulled up surveillance footage of the three troublemakers. He watched them sit and plan at the facility. What were they planning? He reached out to the surveillance team and had their numbers pulled so that he could listen in on their phones—even though he knew Joel would already be doing this. He wanted to listen for himself.

They spoke of a man named William and how Silas was William. Jason smiled, glad he got rid of that rat when he could.

As the night grew darker, he watched them, his mind coming up with schemes. Jotting down notes, he made a list of all the weaknesses and vulnerabilities he could exploit. His obsession with them only intensified. He knew his control over the time machine was within reach, and he couldn't afford any obstacles in his path.

Eventually, he received a text from his wife.

"When are you coming to bed? The girls missed you at dinner."

This snapped him back to reality. He sighed, put away his notes, and left, heading back to his room. When he walked in, his wife was lying there reading her book, and he sat at the edge of the bed.

"Where have you been?" she asked. "I feel like we haven't seen much of you in these last few days. I worry about you."

"Can't you see that I'm busy?" he snapped. "I'm busy trying to make this all better for everyone!"

Her eyes widened, fearful, which brought him back to his senses.

"I'm so sorry," he said, his voice softer. "It's just been really stressful lately. I didn't mean to snap at you like that, honey. I mean it."

"You seem different," she told him. "There is something off about you. It's almost like I'm losing my husband, and I'm not able to recognize you most days."

He looked back at her. "I'm still the man you fell in love with."

"No. You're not. But that isn't usually a bad thing. It's a good thing you've changed from the man before. Because let's be honest: he was kind of a dumbass. But lately, you aren't him. Not the changed man. You're much different."

Jason King's gaze shifted from his wife's concerned eyes to the dimly lit room. The weight of his secret plots bore on him, causing his once bright and vibrant eyes to dull. Now clouded with a darkness that mirrored the depths of his ambitions.

"I promise it's just the stress from the job, honey," he said, attempting to reassure her.

She sighed, worry etched across her face. "I just want my husband back," she whispered.

His heart ached as he looked into her eyes, realizing the chasm that had grown between them. He longed for the simpler days—when their love was uncomplicated. But he couldn't turn back now. He had come too far.

With a heavy heart, he leaned in and kissed his wife, trying to bridge the emotional distance that had grown between them. But deep down, he knew the path he had chosen would only lead to further estrangement. Yet he could never let go of his grand vision. His own twisted sense of destiny rested in his hands.

In his dream that night, Jason ruled over a world with absolute power. The people adored him, and his every command was followed without question. The weight of his authority pressed upon him, but he relished the sensation of control it brought.

He reveled in the supremacy.

Yet amid the grandeur, a nagging feeling tugged at the edges of his consciousness. Something was amiss. A disquieting presence that he couldn't quite pinpoint.

As the dream unfolded, unease grew among the people he ruled. Whispers of rebellion reached his ears. The once unwavering loyalty of his subjects seemed to wane. His absolute power crumbled, and he was left with a haunting emptiness.

He awoke with a jolt, drenched in cold sweat. His wide blue eyes looked around and found himself in his bed. It was just a dream. He decided to take a cold shower, and after, he returned to bed, falling back asleep.

The dreams did not return.

The next morning, he tried to act like his old self. Sweet-talking his wife and taking the girls for breakfast. However, the need for power kept growing.

Joel called.

"Jason, just wanted to let you know that they're meeting with one of the cult members in two days," he said. "Jesse used his wife, who is friends with the member. Meeting at a PTA meeting."

Jason remained silent for a moment. "Go to the bread factory and make sure it gets done today."

"Yes, sir," Joel said firmly. He then hung up.

"Bread factory?" his wife asked, breaking his reverie.

He had forgotten he was sitting with his family. "Yes. A bread factory. Apparently, that cult terrorist group is at a bread factory. They finally got confirmation that they'll be there today, so I was wanting Joel and Control to bring them in for questioning."

She nodded. "Tell Joel not to hurt anyone. I know he has anger issues."

He chuckled. "I will tell him."

Later that day, he received a call from Joel, confirming the successful operation at the bread factory. He didn't press for details; he just needed to know the threat was neutralized.

With that concern addressed, Jason shifted his focus to the time machine. He instructed Joel to arrange a test and informed him that he would be present to witness it.

Upon arriving at the factory, the team let him in as usual. He met with Joel and inquired about the test subject. Joel pointed at a man named Phil.

"Well, let's get going," Jason said.

They proceeded to strap Phil into the time machine.

Cindy stepped forward. "We're going to send him back one year, picking someone at random. Here's the thing they probably didn't tell you, sir: the only way to get back is to take your own life or become unconscious. We don't know why, but this is what the original three had found."

"Okay," Jason said. "Let's proceed."

And so, the test began.

The atmosphere grew tense as the machine powered up. Jason watched intently, his eyes locked on Phil. He couldn't help but feel a sense of excitement mixed with trepidation.

As the machine hummed, and the room filled with a faint, otherworldly glow, Phil's expression shifted from curiosity to unease. The reality of what he was about to experience weighed on him.

Cindy operated the controls with precision. The machine whirred and whizzed, and a low, resonating hum filled the room. Phil went still.

"Is that it?" Jason asked.

"Yeah," she said. "It just looks like he's asleep. We told him to bury something outside, which we will give him some time to get there."

They waited for about an hour. Then another hour passed with no sign of Phil. In the third hour, there was a deep gasp, and Phil sat straight up, panting.

"Welcome back, Phil," Cindy said.

"Yeah, yeah. Welcome back," Jason said. "So, did it work?"

"Well, let's go check." She turned to Phil. "Show us where you hid it."

Phil fell when he tried to stand, so they put him in a wheelchair and rolled him outside. He pointed at a patch of grass that had not been disturbed. Someone brought out a small gardening shovel, and they dug until they found a shoebox. Inside was a newspaper article, some expired chips, and a photo with a signature on the back of a strange man who Phil said was the person he had taken over during his journey.

"Well, this proves that he was here one year ago," Cindy said.

This was it. Finally. It was all coming together.

"Perfect," Jason said. He looked over at Joel. "Do we know when and where the meeting is?"

"Yes, sir," Joel said.

"Perfect. Do we have a way into the meeting?"

"Yes, sir. We have found Katherine's information—that's the person they're meeting—and her butler."

"Wonderful." Jason turned to Cindy. "Get it set up for one hour and hook me in."

"But, sir, the machine needs to cool down," she said.

"I couldn't care less!" he yelled. "Do this now, or I'll replace you!"

"Yes, sir," she replied with a tremble in her voice.

She quickly moved to set the machine up, her hands trembling as she worked. The urgency in his voice left no room for error, and she knew the consequences of failure could be dire.

As the machine powered up again, Jason's anticipation grew. He couldn't help but imagine the possibilities that awaited him once he had complete control over the time machine.

Joel, on the other hand, noticed the change in the president's attitude. But he didn't mind. He had been wanting the president to quit with the kindness. This transformation *was* swift though, and he saw the power consuming him. Still, he shrugged it off.

Cindy finished the preparations. "We're ready, sir."

Without a word, Jason lay on the table, and they hooked him up to the machine and inserted IV bags.

"All right, sir," she said. "We will go ahead and start it up. Just remember: to come back, you'll have to—"

"I know, I know," he said. "Death or knocking myself out."

They turned on the machine, and it hummed.

Jason was out. Darkness. Pressure pressed against his face and chest. His vision then slowly cleared.

"John, are you okay?" a woman in green asked.

Jason looked around, confused. "Huh?"

"You okay, John?"

"Oh, yes. I'm okay. I lost my balance. I'm sorry."

She gave him a worried look. "Okay. Well, our guests will be here any second. Make sure to have the food and drinks ready."

"Yes, ma'am," he replied, realizing he wasn't in his body anymore.

She left the room to meet the trio outside. He followed the other two maids into the kitchen. Voices traveled in the other room as the trio entered on the other side of the swinging doors.

Then there was his cue from the woman in green. He walked out with the two maids, carrying the drinks, and set them on the table. He then went back into the kitchen and listened to their conversation. After a while, the woman asked for a piece of paper and a pen. He walked out, handed it to her, and watched her write down an address, which was in Louisiana.

He smiled. This was it. He did it.

He went back to the kitchen, trying to remember how to get back. It didn't take long before it hit him.

He grabbed a sharp kitchen knife, sliced his throat, and

collapsed. His vision went black. Pressure released from his neck. The last thing he heard was a scream.

Then nothing.

No feeling. No sight. No sound.

But sound soon returned—the sound of people moving and the machine humming. He slowly opened his eyes, everything blurry. Lightheaded, he sat up.

"Are you okay, sir?" Cindy asked.

"I know where they will be and when." He looked at Joel. "Go get them."

The Eighteenth Chapter: The Never-ending Road

Scarlet, Silas, Jesse, and Amelia put the last few bags up the vehicles Scarlet had set up for the trip to DC, making sure everything they needed was securely stowed. It was going to be a long drive—roughly fifteen hours, not including stops. They had planned to take turns driving while the others rested.

As they prepared to depart, Scarlet couldn't help but look around at the place she had called home for so long. Despite her complicated relationship with her father, leaving everything she had known behind for this mission felt surreal. She took a deep breath and reminded herself that she was doing this not just for herself but for the greater good.

With the vehicles fully loaded, they gathered for one final briefing. Scarlet emphasized the importance of staying vigilant and keeping their communication secure. The fate of the time machine—and potentially the world—rested on their shoulders.

Once the briefing concluded, they climbed into the vehicles, ready to embark on their journey. The engines roared to life, and with determination in their hearts, they set off.

Silas took the first turn behind the wheel with Amelia in the passenger seat and Scarlet and Jesse occupying the back seats. The conversation was sparse, and the silence grew heavy, prompting Amelia to break it by playing music. This sparked a lively debate about music genres with her arguing that punk was superior to country, while Jesse held the opposite view. Scarlet chimed in, claiming that both country and punk paled in comparison to metal. Silas, content with being a part of a regular conversation again, simply listened and enjoyed the banter.

As they continued their journey, they made a stop in Memphis to fill up on gas and use the bathroom. Resuming their drive, it was now Amelia's turn to take the wheel. The afternoon sun bathed the landscape, and Jesse fell asleep in the back.

A few hours later, Jesse took the wheel after refueling the car. They drove through the night, and the city lights faded into dark highways and open countryside. The moon cast an eerie glow over the fields and forests they passed, and the engine's rhythmic hum, along with the occasional passing car, were the only sounds.

In the back of the car, Amelia had her head resting on Silas's shoulder. "How are you feeling?" she asked, her gaze fixed on him.

He had been looking out the window and into the darkness but now turned toward her. "I would be lying if I said I wasn't nervous. We don't know what will happen. But I think as long as we have each other, Jesse, and our new friend Scarlet, everything will work out."

She smiled, closed her eyes, and drifted off to sleep.

Scarlet turned around, looking at him. "Friends, huh? Who would've thought? I never would have thought I would be sitting a few feet from you guys, trying to take on the president.

Even with that time machine of yours, you could never have seen this." She laughed and turned back around with a smile.

Jesse kept his focus on the road. He had his caffeine and headphones on, listening to what Silas thought was music. However, it was actually home videos of his wife and daughter. The video he was currently listening to was from last year's Christmas. He sat there with a smile on his face, but underneath, he feared for his wife and daughter. A single tear fell from his left eye, unnoticed by the others.

His shift came to an end somewhere in Bristol, Tennessee, their second-to-last stop. They filled up the car once again. This time, Scarlet would drive the rest of the way. They had taken their time driving on the back roads up to this point, but from here on out, they needed to take the main highway to make up for lost time.

Scarlet merged onto the highway with a sense of purpose. She had a long stretch of driving ahead of her. She drove toward the rising sun, toward the never-ending destination.

City after city, small town after small town, they pushed on.

Amelia, who had been reflecting since she had woken up, broke the silence. "It's hard to believe how far we've come in such a short time. From discovering the time machine to forming this unlikely alliance. Now to confront the president."

Silas nodded. "It's surreal, but it's also a testament to the strength of our convictions. We can't let fear or doubt hold us back now."

She looked up at the front, toward Scarlet. "Do you think we can remain friends or at least acquaintances after all of this?"

Scarlet pondered this question. Could they? Should their beliefs get in the way of a friendship? She looked at Amelia through the rearview mirror and smiled. "I think that can be arranged."

As they continued their journey, the sky brightened in the east, and the highway stretched endlessly before them. The weariness of the long drive faded, replaced by a growing anticipation of their impending mission.

"So where are we meeting the Arlington team again?" Jesse asked.

"We are meeting them a few miles away at a safe house owned by a local," Scarlet responded. "We will be there a day before we go in; we don't have time to sit around and wait."

They nodded.

It was getting close to noon when they made it to Washington DC, and their nerves rose. They had decided to wear surgical masks when they entered the area as this was one of the most heavily watched cities in the country. Cameras were everywhere.

The president's factory was close to the White House, located in an area of Washington known as Langdon. The house they were staying in wasn't too far away, near the US National Arboretum.

They passed over the Potomac River and drove past the White House, shuddering at the thought that President Jason King was somewhere inside. Upon arriving at their safe house, they noticed a few cars already parked there, and a man named Terry greeted them, giving them all a hug and bringing them inside.

The safe house was a cozy suburban home, a stark contrast to the bustling city they had just left behind. It provided a sense of refuge from the impending mission.

Inside, Terry introduced them to the Arlington team members who were already there. The trio noticed that the

Arlington team each had a pistol on them.

The team leader extended her hand to each of them. "Welcome, everyone. We've been briefed on the situation and are ready to assist in any way we can."

The group settled into the living room, and Terry prepared some refreshments. They discussed the plan in more detail—with maps and documents spread across the coffee table. The tension in the room was palpable, but there was also a strong sense of unity.

As they delved deeper into their strategy, with people chiming in with several approaches, Terry's phone rang.

He answered it. "It's for you, Scarlet."

She took the phone, had a brief conversation, and then hung up. When she turned back around, she found all eyes on her.

"My inside source informed me that the captain of Control has left with a group of people," she explained. "They departed yesterday and are headed to our original meeting place in Louisiana. So, that's a good thing. If we proceed as planned, he shouldn't be there tomorrow when we go for it."

A collective sigh of relief swept through the group.

Amelia nodded. "That's great, but we still need to be prepared for anything. We can't underestimate the remaining Control officers. They might be on edge without their leader around."

"We should stick to our plan but be ready to adapt if things take an unexpected turn," Silas added. "We can't afford any slipups at this point."

Everyone agreed.

For the rest of the day, they planned, prepared, and studied the plans. The trio's main mission was to take down the machine and erase the computers while the others protected them.

They sent a message out to any member in the surrounding area to protest at the bread factory, starting at six p.m. Right after the tours ended. That would give the president enough time to finish up for the day and go be with his family. Scarlet's plan was to leave the secretary's office after the tours ended and head to where her mom and sisters were. By the time Jason made it there, the protests would start. That should distract the Control officers stationed there, allowing Amelia, Silas, Jesse, and a few members of the Arlington team to enter the bread factory and carry out what they needed to do.

They made a plan B and C just in case. There wasn't a lot of wiggle room, but it was their best option.

They all left for bed prepared but uncertain of what the next day would bring.

The Nineteenth Chapter: The Light in the Shadow

Amelia woke to the sound of someone making breakfast in the kitchen. She decided not to wake Silas just yet and walked toward the noise, where she found Terry preparing breakfast sandwiches for everyone.

"Thank you for letting us stay here and providing meals for us, sir," she said. "Why would you do this for someone who goes against your beliefs?"

"You're very welcome, ma'am." He turned around with a big smile. "I don't judge people for what they believe. It is my pleasure to help those in need. At the end of the day, we are all people.

"And I believe that care and love for others trumps beliefs. So, even if you were the most hateful person, if I had a chance to show you love, compassion, and care and if that left a mark on your soul, then maybe—just maybe—that care and compassion will come out of you years down the line, and you'll show that to another person in need. Plus, what the president is doing and what he wants to do isn't nice, so that's another reason."

Amelia sat there with a smile.

"Here. Have a sandwich." He handed her a breakfast sandwich.

As she ate her breakfast, Silas walked into the kitchen. He stretched and sat next to her. Terry handed them both a coffee and him a sandwich, and they enjoyed their breakfast.

Terry turned to look at them with a smile. "You two are a beautiful couple. I want you to remember this: communication. Never go a day without telling one another that you love each other, especially in the morning and when you get home. Never forget to do the little things together. And if you get into an argument, never point fingers. If you feel like you're going to yell, take a deep breath and come back to it. Be open to the conversations and never shut each other down. With that knowledge, you will be happier than most couples."

As they sat there, pondering the advice Terry had shared, Jesse walked in, followed by Scarlet. Over the next thirty minutes, the others trickled in. They all ate and helped clean up the kitchen.

The rest of the morning consisted of a refresher of the plan. Scarlet reached out to the locals to get a list of how many would be showing up. She got a count of forty-five people, which was more than what they had thought.

As noon approached, it was time for her departure. They all wished her the best of luck. She reciprocated their well-wishes and set off on her mission.

As the day progressed, they decided to take some time for themselves before the evening's events. Some chose to rest and conserve their energy, while others engaged in quiet conversations.

Terry received a text from Scarlet, confirming that she had made it to the secretary's office without encountering the president.

Jesse used Terry's phone and talked to Sandra one last time.

She assured him that she would be praying for him and hoped that everything went well. A tear ran down his face.

In the evening, Terry walked in and announced, "It's time. The vehicles will be here in a few minutes. I got word that the distraction protesters are on their way." There wasn't an ounce of fear in his calm voice. "It'll take us ten minutes to get there, and once we arrive, we'll have twenty minutes to do what we need to do."

The members grabbed their weapons, and someone handed Jesse, Amelia, and Silas their gear filled with torches and tools.

As the vehicles pulled up, they headed to the front door and got in. Butterflies filled Silas's stomach as his nerves overflowed. Amelia put her hand on his leg and then held his hand. She also kissed his cheek, which helped ease his nerves a bit.

Jesse looked over and laughed. "Don't worry. You don't have to do that for me."

Silas and Amelia chuckled.

She still leaned in and gave Jesse a peck on the cheek in a friendly, loving way. "You'll be back with Sandra this time tomorrow. I promise."

He smiled back and nodded.

Not a single person spoke on the way. The only sounds were the hum of the motor and the tires on the asphalt. At their designated location, they parked the vehicles and sat in silence. The twenty-minute wait felt like hours to them.

Terry, in the front seat, turned around. "It's time to do what you need to. I'll be here with the vehicles, waiting for your return."

The trio got out of the vehicle and followed the rest of the Arlington crew to the bread factory. Thankfully, it was just one block away. They could hear the protesters chanting and yelling outside of the facility long before they turned the corner and saw them.

So far, the plan was looking good.

They made their way up to the protesters to blend in. After a few more minutes, more Control officers, armed with only batons and a few pistols, came out of the building since the two at the gate couldn't keep the protesters quiet.

"NOW!" someone yelled.

The protesters stampeded toward the officers, pushing them down and knocking them over.

"Go!" one protester yelled.

Silas, Jesse, and Amelia rushed into the facility. Inside, they were amazed by how many researchers and computer scientists there were. The researchers and computer scientists tried to physically stop the trio from going any further, but a few from the Arlington team who had also made it inside flashed their weapons.

A woman stepped forward. "Stop! You don't know what you're doing!"

Silas paused, recognizing her as Cindy.

"We are here to stop the president from doing this," Jesse said. "He can't get away with what he is planning."

"I can't allow you," she replied. "You don't know what control he has over us. He will *kill* us."

Silas stepped closer. "Cindy, we have to do this."

"H-how do you know my name?" she asked, baffled.

"Because it's me. Well, you know me as William."

"What? How?" she asked. "How can I trust what you say?"

"I told you I like cribbage at the hotel." He continued to explain how he knew it was her and what had happened to

William, detailing what the president had done to him.

She stood there in shock. As the gravity of Silas's revelation sank in, she looked around at her colleagues and realized that many were starting to question their allegiance to the president. The shock and doubt in their eyes were palpable.

Amelia stepped forward. "We're not here to harm anyone. Our mission is just to stop the president from misusing the time machine."

One of the computer scientists spoke up. "What do you need us to do?"

"We need your help to disable the time machine and erase the data," Silas replied. "If we succeed, it will prevent any further manipulation of the past."

Cindy hesitated for a moment but then nodded. "Okay. I'll help. But we need to act quickly before the president returns."

"Don't worry about the president," Jesse said. "We have that covered."

"How?" she asked, curious.

"As I said, don't worry about it," he simply replied.

She didn't question it further, and everyone proceeded to work. They still acted quickly because they didn't know if Control would send for backup or not. A sense of excitement and power grew as they took down the machine and deleted files.

A single gunshot outside pierced the building, causing everyone to freeze.

The room fell silent. No immediate additional shot followed after a few moments, so they cautiously resumed their work.

Then another gunshot rang out a few seconds later. Followed by several more in quick succession. A cacophony of gunfire filled the building, and fear gripped their hearts.

The Twentieth Chapter: The Shadow Taking the Light

The office door swung open, making Scarlet jump.

"Are you ready?" the president's secretary asked. "The tour is over. Let's go and stay close to me."

Scarlet walked over to her, and the secretary grabbed her hand. They sped walked down the hallway, through another door, and down another hallway. They stopped just outside the double doors.

"Your mom is in there, along with your sisters," the secretary said. "He will be here soon to go get dinner with them. I wish you the best of luck." She then hurried off.

Scarlet froze, her breathing ragged. She had forgotten what she was going to say, but she had no time now to think.

Slightly opening the door, she heard laughter. She closed the door behind her and walked down the hall, passing pictures of her family. But not a single one had her in it. Her heart ached.

She followed the laughter to the second door on the right. It was cracked open. She peeked in. A woman sat there on the bed with two girls, coloring. So happy in their perfect family without her.

She proceeded to walk into the room.

One of the girls looked up and stopped laughing, a confused

look on her face.

The woman looked up and saw the child's confused expression. She turned around, expecting to see her husband coming home early. "Hey, honey. I wasn't—"

She froze when she saw Scarlet's face. Her face turned pale as if she had seen a ghost.

"Hey, Mom," Scarlet said.

"She's not your mommy," the confused little girl said. "She's our mommy."

Scarlet rolled her eyes.

"You're alive…" Sarah said. Tears welled in her eyes. She couldn't believe it. "What…what are you doing here? *How* are you here?" She rushed toward Scarlet, embracing her. "It's really you! You're alive!" Tears streamed down her face.

Scarlet returned the hug, feeling a mixture of relief, joy, and sorrow.

Her two younger sisters sat still, still processing the unexpected reunion.

"Is she really our sister, Mom?" one asked.

Sarah nodded with a tearful smile. "Yes, she is. This is your big sister, Scarlet."

After a few minutes, Scarlet snapped out of the emotional return. "So, no photos of me anywhere? Did y'all even miss me, Mom? Or should I just call you Sarah?"

Her mom stood there—shocked. "Of course, we missed you, honey. We looked all over for you. I didn't sleep for *months*."

"But to edit and get rid of me from the photos? I really was never good enough for you or Dad."

"What do you mean not good enough? You were my light."

Footsteps sounded nearby, getting closer, and a voice spoke from outside the door.

"Who's ready for dinner?" Jason asked. He entered the room, stopping in his tracks as he stared at his long-lost daughter. "What are you doing here?" His voice turned stern. "Why have you come back?"

"Figured that's what you would say," Scarlet said. "No 'I missed you.' No 'I love you.' Not even a hug. Already irritated because you see my face."

The tension in the room was palpable.

"Jason, please," Sarah implored. "Let's talk about this calmly. We have a chance to rebuild our family."

Scarlet maintained her composure, meeting her father's relentless gaze. "I didn't come here for a fight. I came because I want answers, and I want to understand why you did what you did."

"I don't know what you're talking about," he replied.

"Oh, don't do that," she snapped. "Don't act like I'm some foolish girl. So tell me why. Why would you be willing to risk the fate of the future over some power ego trip?"

"Not here."

"No. We are having it here." She glanced at her mom and sisters. "They don't even know, do they? Your whole life—ever since you started this career—has been about *power* because your ego is so massive. That's why I left. You shoved me out of your lives. I remember all the photos you would not let me be in. All of the trips where you would leave me at home. Because I didn't fit the narrative."

"No, that isn't true, honey," Sarah said.

"Quiet, Mom. This isn't your fight. Dad needs to own up." She glared at him. Her voice took on a demanding tone. "Look at your wife and daughters and tell them that I am lying. Tell them I've lost my mind. That I should be locked up in a room with padded walls."

The twins were quiet. So was Sarah.

"Fine," Jason said irritated. "You're right. I despised you. You always wanted to do things your way, ever since you were a baby. I knew you would grow up to be a failure. And I was right about that too. I followed you, tracked you. Because, well, I have the power to. I know everything you have been up to since you left."

"Why would you when you hated me?" Scarlet said. "What is the point?"

"Well, here's the thing. Just because I couldn't stand being around you doesn't mean I wanted you dead. I had to make sure you were alive in case you came crawling back for your mother." He pointed at Sarah, who was still in shock.

"But you never helped when I was struggling. Never mentioned to Mom that I was still alive. You kept this to yourself?"

"You're correct. I couldn't care less about how you struggled. You weren't my problem anymore." He sighed, looking at his watch. "I knew you were coming back today, but you did catch me off guard with the timing. Let me guess. Your insider was my secretary? Yeah. She's being dealt with now. Oh, and don't worry about Silas, Amelia, and Jesse. They'll be taken care of as well."

"So, you're willing to kill all these people over some ma-chine?" Scarlet asked as she reached for her phone to warn the others.

"I wouldn't do that if I were you," he said in a condescending voice. "You see, you all thought you had the upper hand, but you don't. Right now, I've got thirty-plus Control officers loaded with whatever they need to take down your team at the factory. I couldn't care less if they kill the people working there. I can always get more."

"You truly are the sick bastard I always believed you to be." She turned to her mom. "See? This is what you've been ignorant of—either on purpose out of fear or just not noticing. But I doubt you're that oblivious."

"Don't look at her," Jason snapped. "You don't have that right anymore, Scarlet. Ugh. Even saying it doesn't feel right. Oh, and another thing."

As she turned toward him, a bang rang out.

A warm liquid spread from her stomach. She pressed her hands to it, and when she pulled them away, she saw blood. "Why?" she asked with pain in her voice.

The smell of burning flesh and iron singed her nose. She collapsed onto her knees and then onto her side as the searing pain settled in. The twins began bawling from the sight, while Sarah was froze.

"Why?" she asked again.

"I have to clean up the mess that was made the day you were born," he simply replied. "Don't take this personally, honey. Think of it like changing your present to forget your past and make your future better."

Two Control officers walked in.

"Take her to the factory and drop her on the curb. If anyone is still alive, I want them to see the mess."

A scream rattled the air—a scream not just from seeing her daughter be shot but from the pain of being shot herself. It just registered for Sarah that she had been hit too. The bullet must've torn through her daughter and hit her.

She wept, not only from seeing her oldest daughter, who she thought was dead thirty minutes ago, shot and bleeding out but for herself. She collapsed.

Panic rose in Jason. His perfect wife had just witnessed what he had done. There wasn't a lie he could come up with to hide it. He called for doctors—anyone to come save her.

Her crying continued as Control dragged Scarlet down the hall and to the garage.

Scarlet's pain increased as they dragged her to a vehicle; her abdomen tore, and her legs went numb from the lack of blood. The guards tossed her into the trunk and drove off. All she could see were passing streetlights. She eventually passed out.

She woke to the feeling of falling. There she lay on the curb, like a mangled bag of garbage. She tilted her head, and all she saw were the bodies of the protesters strewn about. Dead.

Jason won

The Twenty-First Chapter: Broken Hope

Gunshots from outside the factory continued to ring, their echoes reverberating inside.

"Don't stop!" Amelia yelled. "Keep going!"

Everyone worked faster and harder. Silas dismantled the machine as quickly as he could. Screams pierced the air from outside.

Jesse ran up next to him to help. "What else needs to be done?"

"Just a few more cables and ports need to be destroyed," he replied.

They moved with speed, having worked on building this machine several times before.

When the gunshots stopped, everyone went quiet. One final shot rang out.

"I got this," Silas said. "Go see if Amelia needs help."

Jesse nodded and ran over to assist her.

A loud boom reverberated from the door.

"They're trying to kick it in!" someone said.

Another boom. And another. Then silence.

Silas hesitated, wondering if they gave up.

But as soon as he thought that, a big metal-type ram burst

through the doors, followed by five canisters that spewed smoke everywhere. People coughed and screamed.

He wondered if it was tear gas but knew it didn't matter. He had to finish. He looked behind him and saw Jesse and Amelia.

"How much is left?!" he screamed.

"Almost done!" Jesse yelled back.

More canisters were tossed in, accompanied by loud popping explosions and blinding lights. Silas lost his sight and hearing. It felt like his eardrums had ruptured, and he fell to the ground.

"Get up!" he yelled to himself.

And he did. He struggled to his feet, still stunned, and surveyed the chaotic scene. The people who had been helping them were disoriented—some lying on the ground, others still in their chairs. All clutched their ears in pain.

He turned and saw Jesse and Amelia. They were also battling through the chaos and pain, their resilience unwavering.

Despite the turmoil, he felt a surge of relief. He turned toward the machine and destroyed one final piece. Done.

His heart racing, he turned toward his friends to make his way to them. Some of his hearing returned. However, it didn't help drown out the terrifying destruction—the relentless gunfire, the piercing bullets, and the agonized screams.

An intense pressure built in his chest, followed by a searing pain in his back. It was a burning sensation, akin to the worst heartburn imaginable. Amelia's penetrating scream was a bloodcurdling sound that cut through the chaos.

Silas didn't initially grasp the gravity of his situation, but as soon as he touched the source of his pain, he realized the horrifying truth: he had been shot.

His right lung had been hit, and his breath grew shallow. Panic surged as he struggled to breathe and coughed up a foreign liquid. His lungs refused to cooperate.

Amid the chaos and his own mounting fear, another searing pain flared in his left thigh. As if he had pulled a muscle combined with the sensation of burning iron coursing through his leg. He fought to stay on his feet, but his left leg wouldn't support him. Adrenaline gave way to excruciating pain.

Amelia's screams continued, her tear-streaked face haunting him.

Despite the dire circumstances, he couldn't help but be struck by her beauty. He longed to scream back to her—to convey his love and reassure her—but his ravaged lungs couldn't muster the breath.

"I lov…" His voice faltered.

A Control officer, wearing a chilling smile, approached him. Silas turned to see a woman screaming and an older man desperately trying to hold her back. He then focused on the man on one knee, blood pooling from his thigh and chest. Without uttering a word, the Control officer raised his weapon and pulled the trigger.

Another shot pierced Silas's chest.

His vision swirled, the weight of his body growing lighter. His sense of smell vanished, but his hearing remained, though useless. All that reached him were Amelia's agonized screams and the relentless gunfire.

As Silas's consciousness faded into the abyss, memories of his time with Amelia and Jesse briefly flooded his mind. He recalled their shared moments and dreams. He knew their actions were paving the way for a better future. Despite the encroaching pain and darkness, he clung to the hope that their mission would succeed.

And then, in an instant, Silas Vale was no more.

Screams were the only sounds escaping Amelia's mouth. Her stomach was turned upside down, her knees grew weak, and her eyes stung from the streaming tears. Her heart was torn to shreds.

She tried to go after him, but Jesse grabbed her.

"NO!" he shouted. "We can't."

She hit him, screaming, but he simply took the hits, holding back his own tears.

She screamed even louder, desperately trying to reach him—the man she loved, the only man who saw her for who she truly was. And the very love she cherished was now being torn apart.

Silas looked lifeless. As if his soul had been drained from his body. She screamed and cried and screamed—eventually passing out.

Jesse, battered and bruised, picked her up and ran. Bullets whizzed by him, one nicked his calf, but he didn't stop. He kept going, jumping over the bodies on the ground.

Outside, he froze, shocked to see that there weren't any police or anyone else in front of the building. But someone was lying on the ground, bleeding out.

Scarlet.

Panic surged through him, driven by pure adrenaline and fear. Despite the increasing pain coursing through his leg, he hastily placed Amelia on his shoulder and grabbed Scarlet's collar, dragging her.

He managed to reach the street corner, where he stopped and gently set them both down. He frantically searched through Scarlet's pockets, muttering, "Where is it? Where is it?" His fingers grabbed her phone, and he used her pale face to unlock it.

He accessed her contacts to find Terry. However, he then remembered that Terry's name wouldn't be listed conventionally, so he opened a secure messaging app and located Terry's contact. With urgency, he called him.

"GET OVER HERE NOW!" he screamed.

Terry swiftly arrived at their location. He parked the vehicle right beside them and rushed out. "What the hell happened?!"

"Not now," Jesse replied. "We need to go. Scarlet needs medical help!"

"What about Silas?"

His voice broke and trembled. "He…he's gone."

Together, they loaded up the vehicle and sped away, leaving behind a harrowing scene at the factory.

The Twenty-Second Chapter: Pain Echoing

After calling the doctor from their group, Terry sped down multiple streets. Jesse had no idea where they were heading. He just knew that Scarlet barely had a pulse.

They eventually arrived at a small emergency room. Around the back, they found the door open, and two nurses and a doctor rushed out.

"Where was she hit?" the doctor asked.

"We don't know," Jesse said. "I just found her like this."

They carried Scarlet inside, along with Amelia, who was still unconscious.

"Is there anything wrong with her?" one of the nurses inquired, pointing her head toward Amelia.

"No, she's just in shock," Jesse explained. "She passed out after screaming."

The medical team placed Scarlet on the examination table and removed her clothing. They found the bullet wound in her stomach and used their mobile x-ray machine to take pictures.

The doctor assessed the images. "Good. It missed her intestines and stomach by a hair." He turned to the nurse. "Go get some blood and a sedative in case she wakes up. It's going to get very painful."

The nurse promptly followed the doctor's instructions.

Meanwhile, Jesse and Terry left the room and went to the one where they had placed Amelia. A nurse administered an IV to her due to her pallid appearance.

Jesse sat beside her, holding her hand, and finally allowed himself to break down, shedding tears. The last time he had really cried was out of joy when he saw his daughter born, many years ago. But now the floodgates opened once more.

Terry approached him, placing a reassuring hand on his shoulder.

Time slowly passed in the small emergency room as they waited for any news of Scarlet's condition. After a while, Jesse, still seated beside Amelia, noticed she was starting to regain consciousness.

"Where is he?" she softly asked, her voice hoarse from the earlier screaming.

He looked over at her, relieved to see her awake. "You're awake," he said gently.

"Where is he?" she repeated.

He hesitated but then softly replied. "He…he's gone, Amelia. He was killed."

Her eyes welled with tears before the tears streamed down her face like a continuous river. She curled into the fetal position, facing Jesse, and continued to hold his hand.

He could feel her pain through her silent cries and her tight grip. "Would you like some water?"

She looked up at him, her red and glossy eyes filled with grief. "I want him, Jesse," she uttered. "I want *him*. Why…? Why didn't you let me go get him? I could've…"

"I know you wanted to." Sadness filled his voice. "I wanted to as well. And if I knew there was a chance we could've saved him, I would've let you go. I would've gone with you. But…but we couldn't…"

She continued to stare at him, her tears still flowing. After a moment, she buried her face into his arm, soaking his sleeve with her tears and snot.

He climbed onto the bed and held her as if she were his own daughter. She wept as he cradled her head, providing whatever comfort he could. She tried to stifle her sobs, and he could feel the tension in her body.

"Breathe, Amelia," he muttered. "Cry if you need to. Don't hold it in."

His own tears flowed—not for his pain but for hers. He couldn't help but imagine what it would be like if it were his own daughter who had lost her love. The weight of their shared grief hung in the room, a palpable cloud of sadness.

Amelia's words cut through the sorrow. "We were supposed to get married, Jesse… *Married.*"

"Oh, honey…" Regret filled his voice. "I am so sorry. If I could change positions with him, I would."

"Wh…why him? Why did it have to be him?" Her voice broke. "I…I can't believe he's gone."

Jesse's eyes mirrored her sorrow. "I know… It's incredibly hard to accept. I know how much he loved you and how deeply you love him."

As they clung to each other in their shared grief, the minutes felt like hours, and the room seemed to grow smaller, suffocating them with mourning.

Amelia's tears eventually subsided into soft, uneven breaths. Her exhaustion from the emotional rollercoaster was evident as her eyelids grew heavy, and she drifted into an uneasy sleep. Jesse continued to hold her, his heart heavy with grief but also with a profound sense of responsibility for comforting her through this devastating loss.

The room remained enveloped in silence. He soon fell asleep while holding her. The hours passed by as they slept, providing the first moments of relaxation since they had woken up that morning.

Amelia dreamed. In her dream, she and Silas were at their wedding, exchanging vows and surrounded by friends and family. The glow of sunlight and the scent of flowers bathed them. But the darkness pulled Silas away.

She tried to chase after him, yet she couldn't move. He was too far. Again and again, he was shot. Their family and friends remained still, mere spectators to the unfolding tragedy. She screamed for them to help, but no one moved. After Silas finally fell, they all stood and clapped.

She woke, drenched in sweat and tears. Jesse still held her tightly. He squeezed her even closer as she cried once more.

Amelia's heart pounded as she tried to shake off the haunting remnants of her dream. The vivid image of Silas being torn away from her left her trembling. Jesse's embrace provided some solace, but the nightmare still clung to her like a persistent shadow.

In her half-awake state, she gradually became aware of the quiet hum of the hospital room and the rhythmic beeping of medical equipment.

"Where are we?" she asked, her voice wavering.

"A small ER several miles away," Jesse replied. "We are safe for now."

She looked around and nodded. "Jesse," she whispered, her voice still trembling. "I can't shake that dream. It felt so real, so...dreadful."

He tightened his grip on her once more, offering a silent, understanding presence. "I know, Amelia," he said softly. "We've been through the unimaginable. But you're not alone. We'll get through this together."

Terry walked into the room. "She's doing okay for now. They were able to fix her up, but she's asleep and needs to heal and rest."

Jesse nodded.

"Oh, Jesse, I hope I wasn't out of line for this, but I did call your wife to briefly let her know what had happened and that you are safe and okay."

He thanked him.

"Well, I have a friend who doesn't live too far from here. They're willing to let you two stay there for a few nights if you want before going home."

Jesse thought for a moment and then turned to him with a grateful expression. "Yes, that would be wonderful. Thank you. I think a hot shower and sleep will help some."

Terry smiled. "Good. I'll go ahead and take you both now over there."

They left the room after they took the IV out of Amelia. Terry updated the doctor and thanked him. Jesse sat with Amelia in the back of the car, noticing that Terry had put a blanket down to cover the blood from Scarlet.

Amelia didn't say or move much after getting into the car.

Terry drove them a few blocks, made a left turn, and parked in front of a pretty nice house. "Her name is Rhonda, but we call her Grandma. She will take good care of you."

As they walked up to the house, the front door swung open. A waft of cookies drifted in the air, and there stood a little old lady, hunched over.

"Oh, honey," she said. "Come in. Come in. I am so sorry for what you have been through."

She took them into a nearby bedroom. Amelia got on the bed, lying in a fetal position, still in shock.

Jesse sat next to her and looked at Grandma. "Thank you so much for allowing us to stay here. Do you mind if we use your shower? I think a hot shower might help."

She nodded with a smile. "Take all the time you want. I'll be in the kitchen with food whenever you're ready." She shuffled out of the room.

Terry smiled. "Everything will get better. Take care of her and take care of yourself. I will arrange a vehicle for you two the day after tomorrow."

They said their goodbyes, and Jesse gave Terry a hug before he left.

Jesse then leaned over Amelia and softly asked, "Do you want a shower or a bath?"

She just nodded.

The pain for her in his heart overwhelmed him.

He went into the bathroom and turned on the bath, making sure the water wasn't too hot or cold. Returning to the room, he gently undressed her and carried her to the bathtub. With great tenderness, he washed her hair as he had done with his daughter when she was little. He then scrubbed her body and washed her face.

"Don't ever hide the pain," he mumbled. "Don't bury it. Feel it, but don't let it take over you. I know this might not make sense now, but one day, it will. So, feel the pain. Cry. Don't care what others think."

He repeated the process a few times, watching as her body relaxed somewhat.

He let her sit there for a few more minutes, allowing the warm water to embrace her. He then grabbed a fresh, fluffy towel and lifted the tub's plug. Carefully, he helped her into a standing position and assisted her out. He dried her body first and then her hair, wrapping it in the towel. He found some loose-fitting basketball shorts and a shirt for her to wear. After sliding the shirt over her head and helping her put on the shorts, he noticed that her eyes and face still showed signs of being lost.

He kissed her forehead and gave her a hug. She wrapped her arms around him and squeezed. Cried a little more. She then wiped her tears and stepped back.

In a whisper, she said, "Thank you."

He gently guided her out of the room and into the kitchen.

Grandma had made chili, and the enticing aroma filled the air. She poured them both a bowl and generously sprinkled cheese on top. In front of each of them, she placed a bowl of garlic bread.

Jesse took a few mouthfuls and sank into his seat, savoring the flavor. He glanced over and noticed that Amelia hadn't touched her food. Pushing his bowl aside, he moved closer to her, intending to feed her, but Grandma shooed him away.

"You eat your food, honey. I'll help her," Grandma said.

She sat next to Amelia and gently rubbed her back. Picking up a spoon, she scooped a small amount of chili and blew on it to cool it down before offering it to Amelia. At first, Amelia refused, but the irresistible aroma got the better of her, and she ate the spoonful. After a few bites assisted by Grandma, she took the spoon from her and fed herself.

Who knew the power of a grandmother's cooking could really heal? Jesse chuckled at the thought.

"Would you like something to drink?" Grandma asked.

They both nodded.

"I have water, tea, cola, orange soda, and milk."

Tears welled in Amelia's eyes.

"Oh no. Did I say something wrong?"

She sniffled. "No. It…it's just that orange soda was, I mean, is my favorite soda. I would love some please."

Grandma promptly fetched her a soda, poured it into a glass, and handed it to her. As Amelia took a sip, the sugary orange flavor rushed through her, bringing back memories of Silas, which made her feel sad again. She picked up the soda, thanked Grandma, and shuffled back to the bedroom.

"Poor thing," Grandma said as she cleaned up the dishes. "It's an awful thing that happened. I do hope she gets better."

Jesse offered to help clean, but she waved him off.

"Go get some rest. Go be with your friend," she urged.

He nodded and returned to the bedroom, finding Amelia lying on the bed, still holding the glass and curled in a fetal position.

"This just reminds me of all the fun Silas and I had together," she mumbled. "The times I spent at his house. What will I have now, Jesse? Who will I make those moments with?

"He proposed to me the weekend we stayed at your house, in the guest room. It wasn't fancy. Just us two. He said he couldn't wait to ask any longer. He said he wanted our friendship to turn into a partnership—vows, husband and wife, etc. But look at me now! I don't even have that. All I have is orange soda…"

Jesse got on the bed and sat next to her, rubbing her back. "You have me and Sandra and our daughter as well. We will be here for you. Always will. You're not going to lose us."

She sighed and took a sip of her soda. A little of it spilled onto her cheek, which she left unattended. "I thought I wasn't going to lose him. Look where we are now…" She placed the cup on the nightstand, rolled over, and rested her head on Jesse's chest, wrapping her arms around him.

He continued to rub her back.

"I don't want to talk about this anymore tonight." Slowly, she drifted off to sleep.

Jesse lay there, holding his friend. Somehow, he found solace in the quiet and the emptiness. After everything they had been through, this emptiness was a welcome respite. And he, too, soon drifted off to sleep.

The Twenty-Third Chapter: Rising after Fall

Blackness enveloped Scarlet, accompanied by the sounds of medical equipment. A heart rate monitor. Someone talking. A pressure pressed into her stomach and back, and something itched her throat. She coughed and tried to open her eyes, but the light was blinding, and she choked. Cables held down her wrists. Yet no pain.

Terry ran to her side. "Scarlet, stop. Don't pull the tube out. You've had a lot of blood loss. We are in an ER, not a hospital, so please just lay there. I'll go get the doctor."

She simply lay there, tears streaming down her face. Unable to wipe her own tears.

Her father had shot her. She knew he hated her but to try to kill her? Who would do something so demonic?

She thought back to that night—the yelling, the arguing. Her father admitting to being disgusted with her since she was born burned in her mind. It hurt her more than she thought it would.

Her thoughts then drifted to her team. Did they make it out? Had her dad killed everyone? Did they destroy the machine?

She tried to stay calm as her heart rate monitor sped up. And she couldn't do anything about it.

Terry walked back in with the doctor, who looked at her vitals and asked her how she felt.

"Well, I think we can take out the tube," he said. "It's not a comfortable feeling, okay?"

She nodded. He then unhooked it and pulled it out. As it slid out of her mouth, she felt like she was throwing up. She gagged, and stomach acid rose into her mouth.

Terry grabbed a glass of water and raised it to her mouth.

She took a sip. It tasted so sweet. She then leaned back and asked, "What happened to the team?"

He sighed. "They were attacked. More Control officers showed up, and most, if not all, of our people died." He looked away. "I went back late at night, and they had already cleaned up the bodies and disposed of them."

"Look at me," she said. "Did Silas, Amelia, and Jesse destroy it?"

He looked into her eyes. "Yes. But…but at a cost. Silas was killed."

She kept a straight face, trying to maintain her leadership status, but tears streamed down her face. "Killed…" Her lip quivered. "I…I could have stopped this. He said he would do this. I should have called or done something, but I didn't."

"Don't blame yourself," Terry said. "They knew the danger and the potential cost of the mission."

She looked away, tears running down her face. "What do we do now? When can I go home?"

"We will figure that out another day," he said calmly, "and I'll ask the doctor." Before he walked out, he turned on the television so that it would drown out her weeping. So she could cry in peace.

The moment he left the room, she bit her pillow and

screamed, crying harder than she had ever cried before. But words from the TV made her stop.

"Madam President is currently in the hospital due to an unknown illness," the news anchor said. "The president is with her and wishes that everyone prays for them. We wish you the best, Madam President."

Scarlet cringed. "Illness?" she yelled. "ILLNESS?! He *shot* his own damn daughter, and the bullet hit his wife!"

Scarlet's anger boiled within her. She couldn't believe the audacity of the White House. Even though she couldn't do anything at the moment, she made a vow that she would make the president regret this.

Terry walked back in. "The doctor said he will release you in the morning, but you'll have to be on bed rest for a while. You can stay with me for the time being."

Scarlet thanked him and accepted his offer.

She ended up falling back asleep. Her nightmares repeated the image of her dad shooting her—over and over again. Followed by flashing images of her friends lying lifeless. She woke up a few times, covered in sweat, and the nurse had to come to clean her wounds as a result.

When morning finally rolled around, Terry walked in. "Are you ready to get into a normal bed?"

She nodded. "Get me out of here."

The doctor came in, checked her vitals, and informed them that she was ready to leave but needed to restrict her walking and be on bed rest for the next week. He handed Terry a bottle of painkillers and antibiotics. He then proceeded to remove everything that was hooked to her and advised her to stick to liquids for the next few days to avoid putting too much strain on her body.

"Yes, sir," Terry said. "I've got it all written down right here and will take good care of her."

With Terry's help, Scarlet carefully sat up and swung her legs over the edge of the hospital bed. Her body had a stiffness to it. He assisted her into a wheelchair. A sharp pain, as if she was stabbed in the abdomen, struck her. As she struggled to stay still, he wheeled her toward the automatic doors.

Outside, the sun was just beginning to cast its warm morning glow. Scarlet took a deep breath of fresh air, savoring the absence of the suffocating hospital scent. She glanced at Terry, grateful for his unwavering support.

In the front, Terry's vehicle waited for them. He helped her stand, which took some time. He offered to lift her, but she waved him off; her ego couldn't take any more bruising. Eventually, she managed to crawl into the vehicle. Even though she denied help, Terry still provided some assistance.

He settled into the driver's seat and started the car. "Is there anything that sounds good? Liquids only."

Nothing sounded appealing until Scarlet spotted a local burger joint that was selling chocolate malts. She looked over at him and pointed like a child. "Chocolate malt please."

He smiled. "Absolutely. But we need to get you something with nutrition as well. We'll pick up some shakes from the store."

She sighed but didn't argue. She was getting a chocolate malt, something she loved but hadn't had in a while.

And for the first time in a long time, someone was taking care of her.

Her gaze wandered out the car window. As she thought over the chaos of the last few days, something didn't sit right. If there was such a wild shootout, why weren't the cops called by the neighbors or even by reporters?

She put those thoughts aside as they pulled up to the drive-through window. Terry placed the order, getting one for himself as well.

She glanced at Terry, sipping her malt. His kindness didn't go unnoticed. How effortlessly he navigated this new, unexpected role of caretaker. She knew the road to recovery would be long and challenging, but with the support of her newfound friend, she felt a flicker of determination deep within her—a determination to not only heal physically but also emotionally and mentally.

"These are pretty tasty," Terry said, smiling. "This is my first one."

She didn't know if it was from the sugar, the comfort of her friend, or the pain medication kicking in, but a buzz of happiness temporarily overshadowed her immense pain.

The grocery store came into view, and he pulled into a parking spot.

"Would you like to go in or stay in the vehicle?" he asked.

She pondered it for a moment. "I would like to go in, but can you get me a wheelchair or something? I don't know if I can walk that far."

He nodded and left the car running while he walked into the store. She watched people go in and out—single people, big families, and new families. Then she saw Terry sitting on one of those automated scooters for shoppers. He was so goofy, zipping around on it, that she couldn't help but laugh. However, it hurt so badly that she began to cry.

He got up and opened the door. "Oh my goodness. Are you okay?"

"Yes." Tears rolled down her face. "I'm just laughing at you.

But it hurts to laugh."

He helped her down into the scooter and showed her how to use it.

She scooted along the parking lot next to him. "I need one of these."

He agreed, saying he needed one as well.

As they entered the store, the cool air and familiar sights and sounds provided a sense of normalcy that Scarlet had sorely missed. Terry grabbed a basket and picked up some essentials.

She watched him, grateful for his thoughtfulness. "Terry, you really don't have to do all this for me," she said, her voice filled with appreciation.

He turned to her, his eyes warm. "I know I don't have to. But I want to. Friends take care of each other."

They went around the store, and he also grabbed some things he needed for the house.

He picked up some fruit and vegetables as well. "I can make you a smoothie at home." He grabbed some ice cream as well. "Who doesn't like ice cream?"

They both laughed at that statement.

He got her some protein shakes and meal shakes, along with some juice and soup. At the checkout counter, she offered to pay but realized she didn't have her wallet with her. He told her not to worry. He loaded up the trunk with the groceries and then helped her into the vehicle. Even returned the scooter to the store.

She sat there, sipping on her malt and just enjoying the peace.

The Twenty-Fourth Chapter:
Homeward

The morning sun shone brightly. Amelia lay on the bed, feeling both happy and sad about returning home. The love of her life wouldn't be there. Would life ever return to normal?

"Good morning, Amelia," Jesse opened the door and said. "Did you get any sleep?"

Sitting up, she bowed her head and shook it. "No. Still having the same nightmare." She had slept the whole night, but her body and mind felt as if she hadn't slept for more than thirty minutes. "How about you?"

He shook his head. "I couldn't sleep. I used Grandma's phone and talked to Sandra. I figured the president doesn't really care anymore. He would've found us by now. Probably busy keeping up with the lie of his wife's unknown sickness." Terry had called and informed Jesse about what Scarlet had told him regarding how everything went down.

They got up and walked into the kitchen, where Terry was already enjoying breakfast.

"Good morning, you two," Terry said. "I figured you two would want to get on the road as quickly as possible, so I brought a vehicle for you to use. All I ask is to drop it off with Katherine; she will return it to me."

They nodded.

Grandma handed them breakfast, and they ate. After their meal, Terry handed Jesse a phone to use for the road. He instructed him that when they dropped off the vehicle, leave the phone in the center console. After they ate, Jesse went to the bedroom and stripped the sheets, and although Grandma tried to argue with him the entire time, he refused and told her it was a nice gesture.

Terry and Grandma followed them out.

Amelia looked back at Terry before getting into the car. "If you find his body, please let me know," she said softly. "I would like to have a body to bury."

He nodded. "I'll keep an eye out."

She hugged him and kissed his forehead, doing the same for Grandma. Grandma magically pulled out a foam ice chest that was filled with leftovers, sandwiches, snacks, and plenty of cookies. Amelia thanked her for the love she provided them.

Grandma gave her another hug. "It was my pleasure. All I ask is that after you grieve, forgive yourself and learn to enjoy yourself again. It's hard to hear, but it helped me."

She nodded and got in the car.

Jesse said his thank-yous and goodbyes and promised to stay in touch. He then got in the vehicle and drove.

As the miles stretched out before them, Amelia and Jesse settled into a comfortable silence, their hearts heavy. She couldn't help but think about the uncertain future. She knew they were on a journey not just back home but toward healing and understanding.

Jesse, keeping a watchful eye on the road, broke the silence. "Amelia," he said, his voice gentle, "I talked to Sandra before we left. She set up the guest room for you to stay in for a few days or as long as you need. We are here for you in any way."

Amelia nodded with a lump in her throat—not just from losing Silas but from how kind Jesse and his family had been.

"Thank you, Jesse," she said. "I'm sorry I haven't been as attentive to your feelings as you have been to mine. You lost him too."

He smiled. "Thank you, but I still have you, and you have me."

She smiled back, and they returned to their silence.

The landscape shifted around them. They passed through picturesque towns and open fields, and the steady rhythm of the road seemed to lull their worries into temporary submission.

She kept looking toward the back seat, still thinking Silas would just appear. But he never did. Jesse tried to distract her by talking about his daughter. He and Sandra were considering getting her a puppy but didn't know where or what to get. This seemed to help get Amelia's mind off Silas for a bit. She talked about staying away from puppy farms and getting a shelter dog because of how lonely and wonderful they are. He agreed.

They stopped at a roadside diner. There, they couldn't help but talk about some of their favorite times with Silas. She talked about him in college and how big of a dork he was. Jesse talked about how he met them and that Silas is still a dork. The conversation was bittersweet.

They then got back onto the highway with the open road ahead. Amelia eventually fell asleep. Jesse let her as he drove on, playing some soft music to accompany the journey.

The miles passed with the rhythmic hum of the engine. As the sun dipped below the horizon, casting a warm golden glow over the landscape, Jesse thought about the bond he and

Amelia had shared with Silas. They had been through so much together. He was grateful for the memories and the laughter.

Amelia stirred from her slumber. She blinked her eyes open and, trying not to let Jesse see, wiped the drool from her cheek. "Did I fall asleep?"

He nodded. "Yes. How are you feeling?"

She sat up straight. "Still the same dreams as before, but I feel a little better."

"That's good."

"Hey, let me drive. You need to sleep as well."

"It's okay," he said. "We will stop for gas and find a place to rest for the night soon."

The moon was high in the sky, illuminating the road. Jesse pulled over in the next town. While filling up the car, he found a hotel not too far from where they were. He got a room for both of them, which had two beds.

"I'll order us a pizza," he said. "Would you like to go ahead and shower?"

Amelia nodded, grabbing the spare clothes Grandma had packed for them. She then went into the bathroom, stripped down, and looked into the mirror. Beside her reflection, she saw Silas standing behind her, smiling and wrapping his arms around her. She smiled, but tears fell.

"Are you okay, Amelia?" Jesse asked from outside the door.

She wiped the tears away and cleared her voice. "Yeah. I'm fine."

"Okay. Just making sure. Pizza should be here in about thirty minutes."

She got in the shower and let the hot water pour over her body. It burned her skin, but she ignored the pain. She felt like she deserved this.

Eventually, she snapped out of it, washed herself, and got changed. She left the bathroom and found Jesse putting his dirty plate in the trash.

"How long was I in there?" she asked.

He looked up at the kitchen clock. "I think about an hour. I didn't want to disturb you," he said, handing her a plate with pizza.

He then showered as well and quickly fell asleep.

The next morning, Jesse woke up and found that Amelia had gotten into bed next to him at some point during the night. She must've had a nightmare.

They checked out of their hotel and continued their journey. The road continued, and the scenery changed from farmland to woods to the city and to the woods again. They finally made it back to Texas late in the afternoon. Thrilled to be back in their home state, they only had a couple of hours left.

Miles flew by, and they were back in Dallas. As they pulled up to Jesse's house, they found Jesse's daughter sitting outside, waiting. He got out quickly, and she ran and jumped into his arms.

His wife came out as well. Instead of hugging her husband, she hugged Amelia first. Tight. After a few minutes, they both let go, and she hugged her husband. She helped unload the car.

For the next few weeks, Amelia stayed with Jesse and his family. She went back home once, only to get some clothes. She debated going to Silas's apartment but couldn't bring herself to walk inside.

The healing process had been hard on her, but she knew Silas wouldn't want her to dwell on it.

She eventually ended up moving back home. They had a funeral for Silas, which brought her some closure. The only thing that hurt her was the fact there was no body in the coffin.

After a month of being home, Amelia watched the president's emergency press conference on the TV, where he announced his resignation due to his wife's illness. The media questioned her sickness, but he ignored their questions. Control had been disbanded as well. Captain Joel had been let go due to allegations made by unknown individuals.

Amelia reached out to Jesse, expressing her desire to return to work. To honor Silas's memory by continuing the important work they had started together, even though it would never be the same without him.

They showed up at the facility roughly two months after they had gotten back from Washington. Amelia walked in late and found Jesse sitting there, working.

"Hey, Amelia, everything okay?" he asked.

"Yep," she replied with a smile. "I'm doing much better."

"How so?"

"Well, I took his last name. We were to be married anyway, so might as well follow through with the name change."

He grinned. "That's good to hear, Ms. Amelia Vale. Well, you'll like this news then. Scarlet called. She's up and walking again. Back home with a nasty scar though. But she's still in this, building up her cult again."

She nodded. "We're back in this."

"One more thing." He grabbed her hand and took her to The Machine. On it, was etched "The Vale Machine."

Tears slipped down her cheek. "Thank you, Jesse," she said.

He hugged her. "It was his design anyway."

They went back to work on their machine, ready to change the world.

The Twenty-Fifth Chapter: Broken Healing

Jesse and Amelia continued their work for the next six months. She wasn't completely healed—and still carried the weight of her loss—but she was feeling more like herself again, putting her focus on her work. Her work had become a source of solace and purpose. She knew Silas would've been proud of their accomplishments, and she was determined to honor his memory by continuing their shared dream.

She and Jesse had introduced new upgrades to The Machine, which were minor but helpful in navigating time travel safely. These upgrades also made it much safer when entering and exiting The Machine.

Additionally, they found a new, larger facility. In this new space, they were working on building three or four new machines, allowing them to assign multiple companies to each machine and reduce the wait time.

As they prepared to meet with several companies they had reached out to, they both agreed that they would take turns time traveling, rotating between the two. They also spent time fine-tuning their time travel technology.

Their dedication and hard work paid off when they successfully conducted several test runs. The results were promising, and they were confident that their machine was ready for practical applications.

Amelia's and Jesse's reputation in the scientific community grew as word spread about their breakthroughs. Companies were eager to collaborate with them and explore the possibilities that time travel technology could offer.

On the day of their first meeting with a pharmaceutical company, they gathered their papers together.

"Are you ready for this?" Jesse asked.

She nodded. "More than ready. I'm excited to finally put this toward its intended purpose."

Jesse and Amelia, in professional attire, headed toward the facility's entrance, having a sense of déjà vu from the day when the president and the captain had shown up.

The company team arrived. They greeted each other, and the presentation began. Jesse and Amelia provided them with a packet that contained information about pricing, functions, and how The Machine worked. They then walked the team through the step-by-step process. They showed them the facility and explained how the control room operated.

When they entered the machine room, one of the team members from the pharmaceutical company asked, "Why is it called The Vale Machine?"

Jesse was about to answer when Amelia spoke up.

"Vale is my last name," she said with a smile. "It was my fiancé's last name before he passed. He was one of the designers of The Machine, and after he passed, I took his name. Jesse here had the wonderful idea of naming the machine after him."

The team apologized, but she waved it off and continued.

"Can we see a test?" one of the team members asked after a while.

"Yes," Jesse replied. "We can show you a test."

They set The Machine up for a small test, going two years into the past. He told them what he would put in a box along with a newspaper from the day he is traveling to as proof. Jesse got into The Machine, and Amelia plugged him in, attaching the IV. The Machine hummed.

"Ready?" she asked.

He nodded.

A click sounded. He fell asleep, and the team clapped. About thirty minutes later, he woke back up, quickly adjusted himself, and removed the equipment.

"Let's check if it worked," he said with a chuckle.

They went outside with a shovel, and Jesse dug up a box. He opened it and pulled out a newspaper with the correct date, a photo of the man whose consciousness he had taken over in front of the building, which had a different name on it, and expired food.

The team clapped and cheered, shaking their hands and accepting their offer. The company even offered to pay them more, feeling that they were charging less than they should, which Jesse and Amelia gladly accepted.

As soon as the company left, Jesse and Amelia tried to stay professional until they departed. However, as soon as they were gone, they jumped for joy, high-fived, and hugged.

"WE DID IT!" she yelled.

"I can't believe they offered more money!" he said. He rushed to the break room and returned with champagne, which they both drank straight from the bottle. "Let me call Sandra! We have to celebrate!"

She nodded.

But as he walked inside the building to call his wife, she

couldn't hold in her sadness anymore. She felt terrible that Silas wasn't here to see this, but she knew they couldn't have done it without him.

"Are you okay, ma'am?" a man asked.

She hadn't noticed the postal worker who had approached her. "Oh, I'm sorry. We just accomplished something amazing."

He smiled and handed her some letters and packages.

"Thank you, sir. Have a wonderful day!" she said, smiling.

He waved and left.

Inside, she put the packages down and flipped through the letters. Bill after bill. Then a yellow envelope with messy handwriting on it. It was addressed to both her and Jesse. Confused, she opened it.

She pulled out a piece of paper, her eyes scanning it. Tears fell onto the paper. The paper shook in her hand. She flipped it over to see if there was anything on the back. Nothing. She dropped the paper, reached back into the letter, and pulled out a Polaroid picture. She flipped it over and screamed, falling to the floor. Crying.

Her whole world crumbled.

Jesse sprinted toward her. "What happened? What's wrong?"

She didn't speak a word. Just silently wept. The only thing she could do was point at the slightly crumpled letter as she clutched the photo.

He picked up the letter.

Dear Amelia, Jesse, and, well, no longer Silas,

Did you really think you could get rid of me? Stop me from obtaining what is rightfully mine? I may not be in the same position as I was before, but that doesn't mean I won't continue to strive for what destiny has in store for me.

You will regret your actions.

I want you to know that I still possess copies of most of the files. It won't take me long to secure the funds and try again. I also have that other file—the one labeled "Future Project."

I apologize that you never had a body to bury. From what I observed, the funeral was beautiful. I hope your meeting today with the pharmaceutical company goes well.

Don't worry. I'll continue to keep a close watch on the both of you. I will be seeing you soon.

Sincerely, Former President Jason King

PS There is a photo in the envelope. I have already hired my first employee.

"Amelia, what's in the photo?" Jesse asked.

She didn't say anything. Just continued to cry.

"Amelia, what is in the photo?"

She shook as she handed it to him. "Silas!"

He grabbed the photo. It was Silas hooked up to a bunch of different IVs and heart rate monitors. Bandages covered all over him. On the back of the photo, it said, "Hopefully, he wakes from this coma soon. He's going to do really well here."

Jesse dropped to his knees. Was Silas alive? This had to be fake. Silas had been shot several times.

"This can't be real, can it?" he asked her, who just lay there crying.

He received a phone call. Scarlet. She asked if he had received a letter too. He told her what the letter said and that there was a photo. She informed him that she had received a threatening letter from the former president, mentioning that he knew she was alive and where she lived. That he was planning to build his machine again.

"What are we going to do?" he asked.

She had no answers.

He looked back over at Amelia, but she was gone. He ran outside and saw her driving away.

Amelia didn't know where she was going. She just drove. Tears blurred her vision, and after an hour of driving, she ended up outside of Silas's old apartment, which was only a fifteen-minute drive. She sat there, staring at the building. She followed a ghostly memory of her and Silas going up to the apartment, reenacting their first kiss. Tears continued to flow.

She was glad that she had continued to pay for the apartment—even after moving back into her own home.

She entered the apartment, which smelled like dust. It had not been disturbed since their last time there together. She sat on his bed and found one of Silas's hoodies. As she smelled it, her tears fell onto the hoodie.

She put it over her blouse and explored his room, finding random drawings in a drawer. They depicted a machine that didn't look like the one they had built. It was labeled "Future." She set those aside and found a letter titled "Dear Amelia." It read:

Dear Amelia,

I know we are only in our third year of college, but you are the best thing in my life. I already bought a ring that I plan to propose to you with. We aren't even dating, but I already know you're the one. I've known for a long time now.

It's not an expensive ring, but it is exactly what I wanted to get you. I remember walking into that jewelry store with you and how you just talked about how pretty it was. It wasn't an engagement ring, but you thought it was just so beautiful.

That next day, when I told you I was at the dentist, I wasn't. I hadn't been there in a few years. I'm surprised you didn't catch on with how hardheaded I am about going to the doctor.

There were so many times when I wanted to ask you to marry me, but I knew I should wait.

I can't wait to build a future with you, my love. You are the other part of my soul, and I am yours. You are worth the wait, even if I have to wait another hundred years.

I can't wait to hear you be called Mrs. Vale.
I will forever love you, Amelia.

Love, Silas

She sat there in his hoodie, holding the letter, as she grabbed her phone to call Jesse.

He answered immediately. "Where are you, Amelia?"

She looked at the letter. "I'm safe at Silas's apartment. We need to get him and stop Jason. We need Scarlet and the cult. I'll be back later."

She hung up.

She looked over to Silas's side table and grabbed a picture frame that had a photo of the three of them. "We will get you, Silas. And we will fix this."

Amelia rose from the bed and cast one last glance around the room, savoring the memories she had shared with him. With the drawings, the letters, and the hoodie in hand, she walked out and locked the door behind her.

Sunrays beamed on her face, enveloping her in their warmth—the same warmth that Silas had once bestowed upon her. She brought the hoodie to her face once more and inhaled deeply, absorbing his comforting scent.

She got in her car. The vehicle muffled the sounds of the outside world. She started the car, and the engine's hum was soothing to her ears. Pulling out of the parking lot, she drove.

"Please be alive, Silas," she muttered. "Come home."

Jesse called Scarlet. "We need to start planning. We'll call you when Amelia gets back."

"I'll be waiting," she replied.

Many miles away, in a hospital room, Jason stood there, looking down at the severely wounded man in the bed. Amid the sounds of the heart rate monitor, the oxygen ventilator, and other medical equipment, as well as the bustling nurses and doctors, he contemplated.

"This is the key," he mumbled. "Healing him will get me where I want."

A nurse entered to check on the wounded man's vitals. "Mr. President… I mean, Mr. King. I don't know what to call you, but visiting hours are over. You need to please leave to let Mr. Vale heal."

Jason looked over at her, shooting her a sharp glare. But then corrected himself with a smile. "Of course. I do apologize. Please make sure my good friend wakes up. It's important." He walked out of the room and headed to his new hideout, where he would begin planning his next move.

The End

The story will continue.

Afterword

I want to express my deepest gratitude to all those who made it to the end of this book. Thank you from the bottom of my heart.

Growing up, I despised English class and writing in general. The rules felt stifling, and the topics seemed dreadfully dull. However, I'm grateful that I rediscovered writing on my own terms. To anyone else who shares my former disdain for writing, I say this: yes, it can be tedious and uninspiring, but it's also what you make of it.

Write something that ignites your passion or simply because you thought, "Fuck it?" Just as I did.

Throughout this journey, I've been fortunate to find a fantastic editor who went above and beyond to clean my work up, English professors who patiently answered my countless dumb questions and friends who unwaveringly supported and cheered me on. In life, genuine supporters are rare gems. Keep your senses sharp and your heart open, for these valuable individuals surround you, waiting to uplift and inspire.

Thank you once again, not just for reading but for being a part of this journey with me.

One last thing, before I let you go on with your day, I have 2 to 3 books already written and or in the works, so keep your eyes open for the rest of this trilogy and for a new story that I am very excited to share. Don't forget to scan the book cover for updates.

Sincerely,
  Austin Brower

Book 2
The Story Continues with:
The Echo Machine.

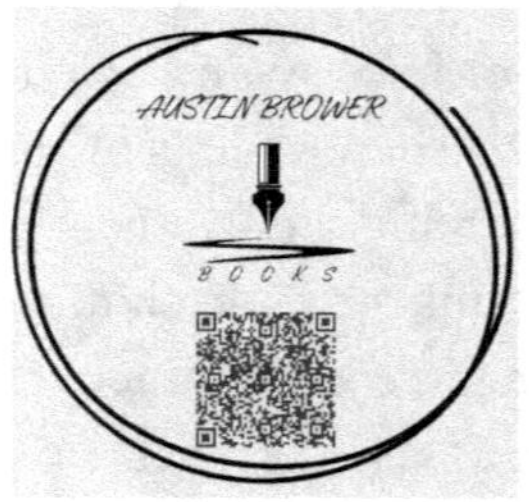

About the Author

Austin Brower hails from Owatonna, Minnesota, but found his true home among the landscapes of Oklahoma and Texas during his upbringing. Settling predominantly in the vibrant city of San Antonio, Texas, Austin has woven his experiences into the tapestry of his life.

After eight fulfilling years serving in the Texas Army National Guard, including a deployment to Somalia, Austin transitioned into civilian life and embraced a new chapter of exploration and growth. Currently pursuing higher education, he is immersed in the stimulating environment of college, where he continues to expand his horizons and shape his future.

Discovering a newfound passion for writing, Austin has found solace and expression in the art of storytelling. Despite being a novice, he approaches his craft with enthusiasm and a hunger for knowledge, eager to refine his skills and share his unique perspectives with the world.

When not buried in textbooks or lost in the depths of his imagination, Austin can often be found immersed in the captivating worlds of fantasy and science fiction literature, where each page unveils new realms of wonder and possibility.

With an open heart and a curious mind, Austin navigates the currents of life, embracing each moment with a sense of wonder and excitement, eager to uncover the next chapter in his ongoing journey of self-discovery.

You can connect with me on:

🌐 https://linktr.ee/AustinBrowerAuthor